Forever Frost

Bitter Frost Series ®

Book #2

kailin gow

Kailin Gow

Forever Frost
Published by Sparklesoup Inc.
Copyright © 2010 Kailin Gow

For information, please contact:

Sparklesoup Inc.
11700 W. Charleston Blvd., Ste. 170-95
Las Vegas, NV 89135 United States of America
www.sparklesoup.com
First Edition.
Printed in the United States of America.

ISBN: 1-59748-899-2
ISBN: 978-1597488990

Forever Frost (Bitter Frost Series #2)

DEDICATION

THANK YOU TEAM FROST for making this second book in the Frost Series come alive. TEAM FROST is made up of so many people who believe in this series and the power of love. To my editors Tara and Jaya, cover artist and designer Darla, publicity and marketing Dorothy and everyone at the EDGE and Sparklesoup – thank you from the bottom of my heart.

To my husband and daughter, thank you for showing me what unconditional love is.

Last, but most importantly, to the readers – thank you for giving Bitter

Forever Frost (Bitter Frost Series #2)

Frost and the Frost Series a chance.
It is because of you that I write.

Prologue

The world of my dreams had become reality. For sixteen years, I had spent every night wandering the halls and towers and gardens of the idyllic Summer Palace, a place of fairy courtship and fairy lore. I had dreamed of princes – charming princes with wintry cheeks and piercing eyes – and of princesses, of gardens perfumed with ripe fruit and flowering plants, of the soft cadences of the Fairy Waltz. Nothing felt more real to me than those dreams – the melody of a dance, the touch of a princess's hand, the whispering thrill of a prince's kiss. And I spent my mornings, my evenings, my afternoons of Gregory, Oregon waiting until it was time to sleep again. I had never fit in among the "normal" girls at my school – the slender, doe-eyed tormentors that are requisite in every saga of teenage angst – I had spent my lunch hour wandering the woods outside the school, whispering to the wind and the leaves and the twigs and branches, instead of shopping at the local mall outlet.

And then I had turned sixteen, and everything changed.

When I turned sixteen, I was visited by the Pixie King with glowing eyes and cruel lips who tried to abduct me, only to be saved by a figure I already recognized – the prince from my dreams. But my salvation was only an illusion; the Winter Court, to which Prince Kian was heir, had been long at war with the Summer Court, which was, I discovered, the land I was destined to rule. And as Prince of the Winter Court, Kian had been charged with stealing me as hostage, using me as a pawn in the political machinations that defined Fairyland.

Over the next few days I learned many things. I learned that things were not what they seemed – from Kian's original standoffish cruelty that morphed slowly into love, to the beautiful forests that sheltered untold dangers. I learned that the Pixie King Delano sought to have me for his Queen, because I was a half-breed – half-human, half-fairy – possessed of great gifts and unimaginable powers. I learned how to perform magic, to connect with the essence, the magical properties within each creature or object and will it to do my bidding. I learned how to transform bread into metal, how to glow like the sun, how to fight – because fighting, I learned early on, was necessary in a world as dangerous as Feyland.

I learned about fairy lore and fairy history, about my own unique place in the Fairy hierarchy. My mother was a human concubine; my father was the Summer King – a liaison that had angered the Summer Queen and I found myself facing almost as much danger from my own nation as I did from our rivals.

Forever Frost (Bitter Frost Series #2)

I learned too that Kian was a brave soldier and a loyal friend, a principled idealist who loved nothing more than his Winter Court except, perhaps, me. I learned that he was an accomplished cook – for men did the cooking in Feyland – and that he loved to paint almost as much as I did. I learned that we had much still to learn about each other, and that his kiss was the most powerful sensation I had ever experienced.

And then there were the bad lessons.

I learned that my best friend, Logan, was a werewolf, a shapeshifting creature that lived between Feyland and the Land Beyond the Crystal River – which they called my world. And, when he was killed in a battle with the Pixie King, I learned that he was a hero, too.

All these revelations hadn't just changed my life. They had changed *me*. I was no longer the shy insecure "loser" Breena who had shut out the world outside her own head in the halls of Gregory High School, knowing that the real world would never match my somnolent fantasies. I was a princess, in destiny, if not in power; it was my responsibility to learn about Feyland – its ways, its secrets, and it's magic. It was the "real world" now – my home, Gregory High, the woods behind the school, were all part of the mythical Land Across the Crystal River in which some denizens of Feyland didn't even believe. It was my responsibility to broker peace between the Winter and Summer Courts – to balance the stirrings of my heart with the needs of a people that weeks earlier I had thought belonged only in the pages of *Causabon's Mythology.*

And today I had to make my first choice as Princess. I had been captured by the Summer Queen – who had revealed to me that I, along with my mother Raine, had been exiled from Feyland; we were dangers to the throne. Now I understood why. My mother was in the clutches of the Winter Court, who wished to use her in exchange for the Summer Court's hostage, Kian's sister, the Princess Shasta. And there was nothing more dangerous – for my family, for my kingdom, than my mother in peril. Raine was my father's great weakness – there was nothing he would not do for the woman he loved – and as long as my mother was in the Winter Court's hands, the Summer Court could be annihilated in a moment by a king who loved the mother of his child more than he loved the Kingdom he had sworn to protect.

And with a glaring smile, the Summer Queen was asking me – *me* – a girl of sixteen – what to do about it. If she did not like my answer, she said, she could easily dispense with me, leave me in the dungeons as monster-bait.

I wanted to be a strong queen, a proud queen – like the Summer Queen – who, for all her hostility, inspired in me a grudging sense of deep respect.

But I was also sixteen years old. And my mother had just been captured by our mortal enemies, a court of fairies who wanted little as much as to make an example of her to bring down the Summer Court.

I had to be brave. I had to be strong.

I had to make the right choice.

Chapter 1

I stood before the Summer Queen. She gazed upon me with a cold, unblinking stare – her eyes as fixed and deadly as the eyes of a snake. She was beautiful, even in her cruelty; her golden-red hair was wound up in a series of knots and tendrils, embedded with emeralds and rubies. The scarlet velvet of her dress hung down from the throne and brushed gently the floor. She looked regal, truly – truly like a queen, and for all that I feared her, I nevertheless acknowledged her authority as Queen of the realm. Instinct led me to want to defend my father and my mother, and yet as she looked upon me, I could not help but feel sorry for her, but take her side. How difficult it must have been for her, to rule a country and fight a war, and all the while endure the indignities of having a husband stray from his marriage and find love with another woman. Did she love my father?

Did I love my father? I had never met him. Until two weeks ago I hadn't even known who he was.

And yet my respect was twinned with an increasing awareness that my life lay in the Summer Queen's hands, that out of caprice or annoyance she could send me deep into the dungeons of the Summer Court as food for the murky-eyed beasts that lived there. This was not a fate that I wanted to meet.

So I began considering what it was that the Summer Queen wanted to hear, what she wanted from me. She didn't want my mother at the Winter Court, where she could prove a threat, where my father would risk all of Feyland to get to her. But no more did the Summer Queen want my mother – or me, for that matter – at the Summer Court, where my mother would serve as a constant reminder of my father's infidelity, of the dishonor that had been brought upon her by the fact that her husband's heir was a child to whom she bore no kindred sense of blood.

Plus, there was the question of the Knights. I had seen the Knights of the Summer Court – brilliant, beautiful creatures with golden wings that looked more powerful than that of any bird, and piercing eyes that scanned the horizon with keen celerity. Any knights used for the prisoner exchange surely would be knights that the Summer Court could not spare from its military campaign; the Summer Court was, I gathered, on the verge of losing, and they could not spare a single body when victory was dangling just out of their rivals' grasp.

I thought, furrowing my brow and swallowing hard. I could feel the Summer Queen's eyes upon me, looking through me, staring into my secret self. I wanted her to know, I thought, that I meant her no harm – that if anything, I respected her all the more for the difficult decisions my family had forced her to make, that I did not want to steal her authority nor her crown nor her husband's love – that I just wanted to stay alive, and for the ones I loved to stay alive, whether beyond the Crystal River or here in Feyland.

Perhaps with her magic she sensed this; her gaze relaxed, and her eyes grew less terrifying in their coldness.

"Well?" she said – but her tone was less accusatory than it had been previously.

"Well," I said, "here's the thing. I'm not going to ask for my mother to come back here. I'm not going to lie to you, your Highness – she's my mother, and I love her, and of course I want no harm to come to her – and yes, your Highness, I'm a child of sixteen and I want my mother with me. But I know enough to know that she is not welcome here in the Summer Court, nor am I. I am happy to go from here, to take her with me, to leave you be – I am happy, if you should wish it, to relinquish any claims to power I, or my family, have." She looked stung to be reminded of it and I wondered if I had faltered here. "But I also know that neither you nor I have an interest in leaving her in the Winter Court. While I hear the Winter Queen has little maternal interest in her children, it is not good politically for the Princess Shasta to remain in our custody, and while the Winter Court does not yet realize the extent to which my mother's presence among them is a political coup for them, they may yet realize it – so we want to make the exchange as soon as possible, before they up the stakes, or demand my father abdicate and give up the Kingdom altogether – and if you'll excuse my saying so, Your Highness, from what you've already said it rather sounds like he might."

"The silly man would do anything for her," said the Queen.

"I can't help that, your Highness," I said simply. "Two weeks ago she was just my mother, and my father was a man I had never met, whose name my mother told me she didn't know. I apologize for the offense my blood carries, but know I bear such a burden unwillingly."

This mollified her somewhat.

"You are Queen in this realm," I said, "and I bow my head to your decisions and your statutes. That said, if I may continue..."

"Continue, yes, girl," she said, with a wave of her hand.

"We need to make the exchange as soon as possible," I said. "But you cannot now spare any knights of the Summer Court; already those you spared to abduct me were lost from the frontier. So let me suggest that I, instead, make the trade."

"You?"

"I will escort Shasta to the Winter Court –

I have a feeling through connections there that they will not harm us." I thought of Kian and hoped I could get in touch with him in time. "Once the exchange has been made, my mother and I will return home, beyond the Crystal River, back into exile, and you need never worry about us again. The Winter Court will be more willing to let us go when they realize we have nothing to do with their wars or their fighting."

"Perhaps," her lips curled into a smile. "If they believe you have no claims on the throne."

"I wish only to remain in good health and serve the current ruler of the Summer Court," I said, bowing deeply.

"Well then," she said, considering. "I cannot deny you have impressed me somewhat," she said. "You speak like a royal, even if you don't yet act like one."

It would get me home safely with my mother and perhaps help the war come closer. And, maybe, just maybe, it meant that I would be able to catch a glimpse of Kian again. The idea of going beyond the Crystal River for good pained me; despite the dangers of Feyland, I had come to love it, to feel at home in it in a way that I had never felt at home in Gregory, Oregon. But I would rather be alive in Gregory than dead or Pixie-bait in Feyland, and certainly I wanted to save my mother's life at any cost. Still, the thought of leaving Kian for good stung me, and some tears rose in my throat and appeared in my eyes.

"What is it, girl?" said the Queen.

I could not tell her about Kian. Yet I raised my head. "I cannot lie to you, my Queen," I said. "I love Feyland; I have come to love it and will miss it. Surely you cannot deny me that. After all, as Queen, you have done so much to protect and preserve this land that is so beautiful, so inspiring. Please take it only as a compliment to your rule."

"You do have the gift of speech," she said.

"I was on the debate team at my high school," I said, "beyond the Crystal River. It was the sort of thing I did."

"Strange place, that land," said the Queen.

"Almost as strange as here," I said.

She conceded the point.

"And what will a fairy princess like yourself do in...Gregory, Oregon, was it?"

"Well," I said to her, bowing deeply, "I'd like to start by staying alive."

Chapter 2

"Well," said the Summer Queen. "I must admit you have some of your father in you after all. Fairy blood." She gave me an arch smile, as elusive as a cat's.

"I aim to serve my Queen," I said.

"You're no fool," she said, "but you're also diplomatic. Certainly better than many of the young chits flocking about the Fairy Court in hope of being made the Summer Court's next main concubine." She scoffed. "But your father wasn't a bad man, you see. Not altogether."

My curiosity was piqued. I realized then just how little I knew of my father – I didn't even know his name.

"Before he met your mother..." The Queen's voice trailed off. "Oh, what a great ruler he was then!" There was a note of warmth and sympathy in her voice. "What a great ruler! He was handsome – he was always handsome – but he had such a regal bearing. The way he held himself. The way he handled royal and court affairs. The way he could light up a room with his smile – if anyone could bring peace to the Summer and Winter Courts, it was your father. He could smile with that inordinate charisma he had, and make every party at the table – from our Fairies to the Pixies – believe that their interests were being represented, that he truly cared about them. It was a very special gift."

"And then what happened?" I asked her.

"Your mother," she said, her lips curling with disdain around the world. "He fell in love, in a way that we don't fall in love in this Kingdom – and now you know why. His duties – forgotten! His cares – secondary! The only thing that mattered to him was interludes in the rose garden and sumptuous diamonds to grace your mother's swan-like lips. And, of course, you –

his beloved baby girl. It made him weak, distracted. Of course, he had the luxury to be distracted. He could play his little childlike games, go in disguise beyond the Crystal River, make eyes at your mother from behind the rose bushes, because he had a wife who was content to sit at home and run the country! Perhaps I was lucky. Many wronged wives have no distractions but their own heartbreak. But I had little time to think of my dishonor or my pain. Instead, I was forced to think of the pain of the whole nation – which your father should have been thinking of, too!" Her voice grew loud with anger.

"I had to protect his reputation, you see, Breena."

She used my name; I couldn't help but feel closer to her.

"Whatever he did, whatever he said, whatever foolishness clouded his mind – I had to stand there with my face to the public and deny it, deny everything. I could not let our king be made a laughingstock. And so I bore my shame and pain alone – allowed my husband to take credit for my victories, my diplomatic treaties, and border-controls, and military campaigns, knowing that the Court could not survive his humiliation made public.

Of course, I was not entirely successful. Ask around in any drunken tavern or bawdy-house and over a few jugs of fairy fruit wine you'll find at least some soldiers willing to bet that something's a bit off with old King Foxflame."

At the sound of my father's name, my heart leaped despite itself! I knew that what she was saying was true – I couldn't help but sympathize with her side of the story. And yet the word *Foxflame* seared itself into my tongue.

She noted my surprise.

"Child, what is it?"

"It's just..." I swallowed deeply. "I didn't

know that was his name."

"What did you think it was, child?" she raised an eyebrow.

I was silent.

"What is it?" And then she laughed. "Do you mean to tell me you didn't know?"

Dumbly, I nodded.

"Oh, you poor girl!" Her former anger was gone, replaced with a regal amusement. "You poor, poor girl. You see, I suppose – when I tell you you are your father's daughter, you must take it neither as compliment nor as criticism, for there is both the good and the bad in him."

"My Queen," I said, "I cannot defend my father, nor can I be held responsible for his actions. But I promise, if you will let me, to try to learn from his mistakes."

I thought of Kian and a great pain, like fire, shot through me.

"You are a good speaker," said the Queen. "Are you good at magic?"

"I've picked up a little," I admitted.

"Enough to keep you safe on this quest of yours, if you decide to go out in search of the prisoner exchange and your mother?"

"Yes, I think so. I know how to fight off Pixies now."

"Good girl," said the Queen. "Pity, isn't it?" She smiled ruefully to herself.

"What is it, your Highness," I asked her.

"I can never have any children of my own," said the Queen. "You are the closest thing to a daughter I will ever have."

I made a motion to speak.

"It is fact," she said sharply, before I could discern any sentiment in her statement. "Neither good nor bad. Perhaps bad. I would have liked children, and you are far from what I would have hoped from a daughter, from an heir. Any heir I could have borne would have been far more beautiful than you, and far stronger. But I suppose I'm stuck with you."

"Make no mistake – if you are to die on your voyage, and your mother with you, to be eaten by Pixies or some such nonsense – I will not fuss. I will not mind. I prefer only that your mother is not in Winter Court's hands by the time that happens. I will in that case encourage my husband to choose another concubine – to create another heir. One bastard is as good as the next." She raised an eyebrow at me. "But you do have fairy blood, Breena; I will not deny that. That much is true."

I wasn't sure quite what to make of this conversation. But at least I wasn't going to be sent to the dungeon, to be eaten by rats and other subterranean creatures. I considered my current position an improvement.

Chapter 3

Once it was decided that I would escort the Princess Shasta through the perilous tangles of forest into the safety of the Winter Court, the rest of the day seemed to pass by in a whirlwind. Guards were summoned; orders were barked. The Summer Queen raised and lowered her hand with an imperious dispassion; she was sending some men to certain death on the battlefields, others meanwhile were spared to perform espionage missions or guard the gates. She performed all her actions, made all her decisions, with the same radiant but haughty calm she had exhibited towards me. I stood mutely alongside her, waiting for her to finish with the affairs of the day, my feet aching with the strain of standing. She did not seem to notice; rather, she made a point of not looking at me as she summoned soldier after soldier in for orders, and I knew that there was nothing I could do more stupid or more tactless than to interrupt her. At last, when the rays of orange sunset had crept like lizards across the floor of the palace hall, she relented and turned to me, peering down her nose with eyes as glowing and warm and all-encompassing as the sun itself.

"You have been patient enough, I suppose," said the Queen. "I have reason to think and hope you have learned at least some manners beyond the Crystal River."

I nodded at her.

"Well then," she said. "I suppose we must get you an audience with the Princess." I was a Princess, too, but she did not acknowledge that. She wanted me to feel small – inferior. Shasta may have been of the enemy kingdom, but in the Queen's mind I had not yet learned my place.

30

"I would be honored," I said, following her lead.

"Guards!" she called.

One of the Fairies entered; I recognized him as one of the Fairy Knights that had stolen me from Kian's side. I thought again of Kian, with his cool beauty and easy manner, and my heart again contorted within my chest.

"Yes, Your Highness." The guard nodded deeply, his knees grazing the lush carpets laid out on the floor.

"Take this girl to the Princess. To Shasta. She will be escorting her back home – to negotiate the prisoner exchange." She breathed out deeply as the guard nodded, rising swiftly and offering me a hand to accompany him.

I followed the guard down the long corridors, remembering that last time I had seen the house of a prisoner of state, I had been on the inside of it – the dank, terrifying dungeon of the Pixie King, filled with darkness so deep, so profound that it had filled my nostrils and my mouth, so strong I could taste it. Was this, I wondered, how the Summer Queen was treating Shasta?

I was wrong. The guard escorted me not to a dungeon, but rather to a room – albeit one under lock and key. The guard unlocked the door and we entered.

The room was sparse, but not spartan – it had the simple charm of a country inn, perhaps somewhat less luxurious than the ornate audience-chambers and throne rooms of the rest of the Summer Palace, but certainly nothing that would have violated the Geneva Conventions over the Land Beyond the Crystal River. Perhaps the Summer Queen's reputation for violence and misdeeds against prisoners had been somewhat exaggerated in the Winter Court – it wouldn't be the first time in my life I'd heard pieces of political propaganda. I had to admit I was relieved. I was beginning to like and respect the

Summer Queen, despite her evident distaste for me, and I had been worried that I would feel compelled to like her a good deal less had I come across the Princess Shasta shackled in irons and chains.

Rather, the Princess Shasta was reclining on the bed, leaning away from us, her hair – tresses so black that they were almost blue – obscuring her face. When she heard the door open she turned towards us, and I gasped.

I had expected her to resemble her brother, of course, but I had not expected the resemblance to be so striking. Next to Kian, Shasta was the most beautiful creature I had ever seen. Her icy stare was unearthly, filled with a power that shook me to the core. Her neck was long and swan-white; her eyes were blue like the sky above snowy mountains. For the first time since I came to Feyland, I began to feel almost as self-conscious as I had in the days of Clariss and her attendant mean girls –

wondering if my arms were toned enough, my nose small and delicate enough, my eyes piercing enough. If girls at the Winter Court looked like that, I wondered that Kian had ever cast eyes on me at all.

"What do you want?" she said, roughly. "Any more news on a peace treaty? None, I suppose. Not as long as you lot are convinced war is the only way to solve your problems." She turned away with a prim scoff.

"Coat on, your Highness," said the Fairy Knight, his voice dripping with sarcasm and disdain. "You're going home."

She blanched.

"What do you mean?" she said.

"Prisoner exchange. You're free to return to the Winter Court at last."

Color sprang to Shasta's cheeks – for a moment it seemed that the thought was more terrifying than thrilling to her. Then she returned to her regal implacidity. "Very good," she said. "Who shall escort me?"

"I will," I said, stepping forward with more bravery than I felt. "I'll escort you."

"Very good," she said. "What are you – I didn't know there were female foot-soldiers among you."

I flushed. "You don't remember me?" I said.

"Remember you?" She shrugged. "I don't remember any of the servants."

This stung; I felt decidedly un-princesslike at the moment.

"If nobody from your Court recognizes any of the royal family, either," I said, "no wonder you're always at war."

She furrowed her brow, confused.

"And I'll remind you that you're speaking to the Princess of the Summer Court."

If this surprised her, she didn't show it. She had been brought up not to.

She made a requisite curtsey.

"An honor, your Highness," she said.

I stared her back down. "An honor, your Highness," I replied.

"You are to escort me?"

"Yes," I said.

"Nobody else?" Her voice faltered for a moment.

"No, nobody, why?"

"Never mind," she shook her head and looked down at the ground. "Let me get my things."

Ten minutes later we had been equipped with weapons and a horse each, and began to set out in the direction of the snow-capped towers and mountains we saw vaguely glimmering in the distance.

"You must be glad to be going home," I said, as we began at a brisk trot.

"I am glad there is progress towards peace," said Shasta, coldly, looking straight ahead of her.

"Look," I said, "I don't care that you're Winter material. It doesn't matter to me. I'm not your enemy. For goodness's sake – we used to play together as children."

"I remember." She kicked the sides of her horse.

"I'm not about to kidnap you. I'm trying to help you."

We came to a small stream.

"Well," said Shasta, through gritted teeth. "Try harder." Suddenly she kicked deeply into the horse's side – setting it off into a canter and then a gallop. It took me a moment to figure out what she was doing – she was going back!

"Stop!" I cried, kicking my mount. "What are you doing?"

Onwards and onwards she sped, darting in and out of trees and clearings like a firefly in the dark. I concentrated all my magic on following her – she couldn't get away – she was the one chance I had of ever seeing my mother again....I bit my lip and held my breath, willing the horse to go faster, willing the horseshoe to push harder against the earth...

At last I caught up with her, grabbing hold of her reins. The horse whinnied and neighed.

"What on earth do you think you're doing?" I asked her. I was in no mood to be polite.

She yanked the reins away from me. "You wouldn't understand...." she said, hiding her face. "Let me go!"

"And risk the lives of the hostages? Not to mention all the people that will die in coming battles if the war gets worse?"

"Stop it," she said, refusing to look at me. "Go away!"

"I won't!" I said. "Now you explain right now what you think you're playing at. I've been dealing with battles and politics and danger for two weeks, and I'm in no mood for someone to play games with me!"

Shasta's face fell instantly. A moment ago, she had been a fearsome princess, with the haughty stare and set jaw of a true fairy creature of a noble race. Now, with a blush creeping like sunrise over her cheeks and tears stinging the almond-shaped corners of her eyes, she looked like nothing as much as a girl like me – *a girl like me.* She looked up and instantly she seemed so much younger, so much more approachable, so much less frightening than she had moments earlier. My insecurities vanished along with my anger; I wanted only to hold her and hug her and tell her that everything would be all right. After all, she must have been scared – as scared as I was – taken prisoner in a hostile land that perhaps she didn't even understand all that much better than I did.

Shasta sensed the change in my demeanor, and she too softened, allowing herself a brave little smile amid the tears that were now proceeding in a military march down her cheeks.

"I can't help it," said Shasta. "It's just – I don't want to leave." She rubbed her eyes. "I don't want to leave the Summer Court. There, I've said it." She swallowed hard.

Not want to leave the Summer Court? I couldn't understand – why would anyone want to stay a prisoner? "What happened?" I asked her, taking her hand; she slowly allowed her fingers to uncurl into mine.

"It's stupid," she said miserably, staring down into the earth. Her tears plopped down onto the horse's main. "It's ridiculous." At last she looked up, taking a deep breath as she did so. "Oh, Breena, it's love."

Love – of course, it was. That power that the Fairy Kingdom feared, despised, tried to eliminate and control and tame. Love – the Winter Queen and Summer Queen alike had called it too great a risk when magic was involved. And here it was again, staring me in the face. I could not pretend I did not understand her.

"Who do you love," I asked her.

"He's..." her voice trailed off. "He's one of you." She looked up at me, pleading with her eyes. "He's a knight of the Summer Court. Please – I don't want to get him in trouble..."

"Your secret is safe," I said. "I know what it is like to love someone you're not supposed to."

"He's called Rodney," she said again. "That's why I was taken prisoner – I did it on purpose. He agreed – he captured me so we could stay together – he brought me my food every day, arranged to be on the quiet guard shifts so that we could steal time, spend moments together – he would have been banished, if the Queen found out, but we couldn't stop."

I felt anger flood my heart. I had tried hard to swallow back my feelings for Kian, to avoid acting on them, lest my responsibilities as

Princess be shirked by my feelings for the enemy. And here was Shasta, putting her entire country at risk – putting *me* at risk – by letting herself be taken hostage into the Summer Court.

"Well, that was pretty selfish of you, wasn't it?" I said. It was petty and mean, and I regretted the words as soon as they came out of my mouth. Shasta looked up at me as if I had slapped her.

"I'm sorry," I said. "It was stupid – please forgive me. I didn't mean to be cruel." I smiled weakly. "I know all too well what love can do..."

"You? In love?" Shasta cocked her head. "But who...how...?"

"Remember the Summer Court when we were younger?" I asked her. "The Fairy Waltz. The promises..."

She clapped her hand over her mouth. "Kian!"

"Yes..."

"Oh, the teasing I'll give him." For a

moment she giggled impishly, like a girl, rather than a fairy – the cares of international diplomacy forgotten for a brief spell of connection. "How did you meet Kian?"

"He kidnapped me," I said. "To exchange me for you. But that rather...it didn't come off too well, as you can see."

Shasta smiled. "Will you see him, when you go back to the Winter Court with me I mean?"

"I hope so," I said. "I don't know."

We began riding slowly again into the night, our spirits buoyed by our conversation and by our connection. "I don't want to start a war," I said, "or make this war any worse. I don't want to hurt anyone. And I've already hurt people because of how I feel. I've already been selfish. I had this friend, Logan, back at school, on the other side..."

"The Land Beyond the Crystal River!" cried Shasta.

"Yes – only he was a werewolf, but I didn't know that until much later. And we were so close – such good friends." The thought of Logan made my eyes prickle with tears. I missed him, on those occassions that I allowed my heart to open up to thoughts of him. "And I think he – well – he had feelings for me. And I had feelings for him too – only then I met your brother...and it was different – and Feyland was different – and I didn't know what I was feeling, whether it was because of magic, or because of..."

"...love?"

"Yes, love, exactly!" I cried, ecstatic to have at last found someone who understood. "And now – Logan was killed by the Pixie King Delano," I said. "So I never got a chance to apologize – for hurting him. I know I must have...for your brother's sake. I didn't mean to. But I was silly, and selfish, and I was too overwhelmed by everything to think straight."

"That's how I felt about Rodney," said

Shasta. "We met in your world, you know. I used to love to glamour – to make myself look mortal – and head into the Land Beyond the Crystal River. I have the magic for that – my mother says I've got some of the strongest magic in Feyland. And I used to go take cooking classes."

"*Cooking* classes?" I was taken aback.

"Yes, of course," said Shasta. "It wouldn't be seemly for a princess to cook here! Cooking is a man's job! Every time I snuck into the kitchen to sniff some roasting boar or fowl the housekeeper would send me back to the blacksmith's hut and tell me to keep forging iron."

I remembered what Kian had told me the night he cooked for me a luscious feast. Cooking was associated with the hunt in Fairy culture – in both the Winter and Summer courts alike. Traditionally, men were the hunters, so men also cooked their meals – the fire was a symbol of masculinity. Women, meanwhile, were expected to forge weapons – they were seen as the givers of life, and therefore also those who should make those items that took life away. It was one of those strange pieces of fairy culture that had not yet sunk in.

"So I decided to try my luck and head on over to the mortal land. And Rodney went too, in disguise, because he wanted to learn recipes – you have no idea how exotic Crystal River recipes are to fairies here. And apparently there's a black market in spices from your world – he would go to the...what was it called? Two numbers..."

"Seven eleven?"

"Yes, seven eleven! And he would buy all of your spices and sell them in our world for bags and bags of gold!"

The idea of my local grocery store providing a treasure trove of bounty made me giggle.

"I found him out – no mortal needs sixty

boxes of cinnamon sticks – and then we fell in love over the most delicious pasta in the world..." Shasta sighed. "Pasta with tomato sauce, basil, and mozzarella cheese. There is nothing in the entire world like it – I'm convinced of that!"

"It's not bad," I said.

"Maybe I was selfish," said Shasta. "But you have to understand – love here is taboo. It's not talked about, not celebrated. If it happens at all it's seen as shameful for both men and women; even if someone felt something like it we'd no more discuss it than we'd discuss our bodily functions or urinate in public! But with Rodney...we could do all sorts of things in your world that we couldn't do here. We'd go on *dates* in glamour – in our mortal disguises – to romantic restaurants! We'd walk hand in hand! We'd kiss in public! And in your world – all these things are not only tolerated – why, they are encouraged!" She sighed. "I think your world has more magic than mine."

"I don't know," I said, watching the sun rise in the distance. I thought of Logan, of Kian, of my mother, of the pain of their absence. "Maybe it's just more dangerous."

Chapter 4

We rode all the way into the dawn, feeling the cool, pink morning breeze pass smoothly over our faces and our shoulders, the first spring hints of dew clustering on our clothes. We knew that it was not long now until we crossed the jagged border – a deep ravine – that separated the warm and tropical lands of the Summer Court from the frozen tundra of the Winter Kingdom. I did not know how I felt; it seemed that Shasta didn't know how she felt either. On the one hand, it was true that I was going into enemy territory – dangerous, cold, fraught with perils from every side and around every corner. I had heard from Kian of the Winter Queen and her often cruel methods of treating prisoners; she was a woman so concerned with honor and bravery above all else

49

that she was even willing to have her own son sent back to the Winter Court in chains for disobeying her orders. And yet with every canter and trot the horses took ahead of us I was one step closer, one moment closer, to being in Kian's presence, wrapped in Kian's arms, the memory of our fairy kiss seared onto our lips. For Shasta, too, her homecoming was a mess of conflicts. She was at last free, at last home. And yet for Shasta home was wherever Rodney was – and so as we rode on, it seemed that she was no less conflicted than I was.

"I'm tired," sighed Shasta, threading the reins between her fingers. "Couldn't we stop and rest, just for a little while?"

I gave her a look of stern warning, but there was no need. She was not going away anytime soon. I had gained her trust, and she knew that as strong as her feelings for Rodney were, running away to him would only put many innocent lives in more danger than they were already in. "I promise, Bree," she said. "Just for a bit."

We camped out in a clearing between two willow trees; I spoke a small enchantment to protect our encampment from harm or sight. Nobody would see us, I decreed quietly, as Shasta and I concentrated our energy on securing the perimeters of our space. Nobody would even get the slightest suspicion that we were there. We were invisible.

"There's a song we sing in the Winter Court," said Shasta. "When we're casting protection spells. It's supposed to make the spell stronger – although plenty of people think it's just a folk-tale."

"Plenty of people in my world think that magic is just a folk-tale," I said.

"Very well," said Shasta. "I'll sing it to you. Kian and I used to sing it when camping out together as children:

When all the world is asleep in bed

51

The creatures resting creatures' heads
Let no peril these borders break
Until the time that we should wake.

I thought of Kian singing – his soft, lovely voice carrying the notes on his lips and tongue – and my heart stung me again. Shasta could tell; she put a warm, friendly hand on my shoulder and smiled at me.

"I think the others are wrong," she said. "You can't have magic without love."

"I hope so," I said, and we settled down to nap.

We were awakened by the sounds of leaves crunching underfoot, and the frenzied whirl of whispers that followed.

"What's going on?" Shasta whispered.

I perked up my ears, then recognized the familiar high-pitched sounds. "Pixies," I said.

We froze. Pixies – I had been captured by them once before. I had no intention of returning to those infernal dungeons again. We knew that the spell had rendered us invisible, but nevertheless we didn't want to take any risks; fear chilled our bones.

"Come on now, Starfeather," cried one Pixie. "We've been walking for three hours – let's take a break, yeah?"

I gripped my sword more tightly.

"This looks like a great spot for a campsite," said the Pixie.

Starfeather shrugged. "It means we won't get our message to the Summer Court until morning," said Starfeather.

"I'm willing to wait," said the first Pixie. "I know how the Summer Queen treats enemy diplomats. How they're treated, or should I say...how they're...*eaten.*" He laughed heartily at his own joke. "I'd rather live, thanks."

What were the Pixies doing sending an envoy to the Summer Court? I furrowed my face in frustration as I tried to make out their words.

"After all, we don't know whether the

Princess is even there!"

"That's what the spies said. And our spies are never wrong," said Starfeather, crossing his spindly arms together and stroking his hand with clawlike fingers.

"The Princess – the stupid bloody Princess! Why do we even have to worry about her?" The rather more indolent Pixie made the executive decision to sit down.

"If Delano heard you talking like that, he'd have you executed," said Starfeather.

"He's crazy about her," continued the first Pixie. "Wants her as his special prize. Hasn't even conducted the border raids or usual robberies and pillagings since she's escaped. And it affects all of us. I've gotten nothing more than some measly emeralds and a hostage or two in days! I need to do some good old-fashioned, state-sanctioned robbery, darn it!"

They were talking about me! I froze, my grip on Shasta's shoulder tightening. What message could Delano possibly have for me?

"Well, once she's back with us," said Starfeather, "I presume Delano's obsession will abate. He'll probably tire of her and kill her before too long. And you can have all the emeralds your heart desires, Dogspaw."

Shasta and I flinched in unison.

"Probably," said Dogspaw. "I hope so. After all, he did tire of the last one."

I didn't want to think about what might have happened to the last one.

"We'll get the Princess Breena back, sure enough," said Starfeather. "Once she hears about our hostage, I'm sure she'll come back out of honor if nothing else. She did last time."

A hostage? I felt ashes in my mouth. Had they gotten hold of my mother, extracted her from the Winter Court, where she was being held? I trusted that the Winter Court would not harm her – Kian would look after her, after all, for although he was loyal to the Winter Court I could not imagine him ever following their strictures so loyally that he would be cruel to someone I loved. But the Pixies were a different matter entirely; I shuddered to think of what they might do to her, especially if they were trying to smoke me out of hiding and convince me to return to Delano's lair and enter Delano's bed.

I squeezed Shasta's hand; she squeezed it back. Between us I felt the spark of friendship, and it comforted me in my fear.

"How will we convince her that the Wolf is still alive?" said Dogspaw. "She won't believe us!"

"She will," said Starfeather, producing a small pellet of fur. "Fur this warm and brown can only be cut off a living wolf."

I gulped loudly, cursing myself for breaking the silence.

"What was that?" asked Dogspaw.

"Nothing," said Starfeather. "Jumpy, aren't you? Just a sound of the wind."

The Wolf – Logan – alive? I couldn't believe it. The last time I had seen him he had been surrounded by Pixie soldiers, their swords drawn and poised, ready to strike, ready to kill. I had already mourned his death, remembered calling out for him in an agonized cry as Kian spirited me away to safety, already been filled with shame at his sacrifice – a sacrifice he had given for Kian as well as for me. And now he was alive? I could hardly allow myself to believe it; joy leaped in my throat, and yet I forced myself to swallow it back down. I was afraid that my hopes would be dashed once again by the machinations of the Pixie King.

But whatever joy I could have felt was squashed quickly by the realization that my cherished Logan was still in the clutches of the Pixie King, a hostage, a prisoner. I remembered my own treatment at the hands of the Pixie guards that guarded that terrible dungeon, constructed out of bones, the stones screaming in pain. They had been relatively hospitable to me – there was nothing to be gained out of damaging a potential concubine, lest any foul treatment mar her beauty. But Logan would have no such alternative; I could easily imagine – all too easily! - that they would have no compunctions about torturing him daily, nightly.

And they wanted to use him to lure me back. I turned to Shasta, my eyes wide and frozen in fear.

"Well, that's enough for now, then," said Starfeather. "Let's have ourselves a bit of shut-eye, eh? We can go see the Princess in the morning. We're not far."

"Not far at all," yawned Dogspaw with a sleepy roll of his shoulders, curling into a corner beside him. The two of them extinguished the fire they had put up, and presently the sound of loud snoring joined in the symphony of crickets that characterized the early morning air.

Shasta turned to me, her whispers hoarse.

"What do we do?" she asked.

I tried to think. "I don't know," I said. "I can't just leave Logan there – but my mother!"

Shasta considered. "You know your mother is safe, yes?"

"Is she?" I looked up at her. "The Winter Queen – your mother..."

"She is harsh," Shasta conceded, "But she is fair. She would not harm a hostage – especially one so valuable as your mother."

"And Kian? Do you think he'd be able to keep an eye on her?"

She laughed softly. "Kian," she began, "would be able to do anything in the world for the woman he loves."

Love me? The idea warmed me somewhat. But I didn't have time to think about that now. My thoughts were for Logan only – Logan who could be languishing in a dungeon somewhere, Logan who could be suffering the agonies of torture, who could be close to death.

I knew that my mother would be safe for at least a little while longer. But Logan had no such guarantee from the Pixies. My choice was clear – to save them both, I had to start with Logan, to return to the Pixie Castle I dreaded so deeply. I knew that this meant walking straight into Delano's trap – I prayed only that my magic had grown strong enough, powerful enough, that I would be able to find my way out of it again. I swallowed hard and concentrated. The one advantage we could obtain, I thought, would be the element of surprise – and perhaps some hostages.

"Draw your sword," I whispered to Shasta.

"What?"

"Draw your sword. Are you willing to fight?"

She drew herself up to her full height, and in her I saw the hint of the Princess who had so intimidated me when I first met her up in the towers of the Summer Court. "I am ready to fight and die as nobly as befits a princess," she said. "I have forged this sword myself."

"Then let us take these creatures as hostages," I said, "and demand that they escort us back to the Pixie Court, on pain of death."

Her hands tightened around her sword.

"Let's do it," she said.

In a flash we left the safe boundaries of our campsite, seizing upon the sleeping pixies, drawing the tips of our swords to their necks. It was not an honorable form of battle, coming on sleeping men in the dark, but it was effective.

"Arise, swine," I said in my most regal voice. "You have been taken prisoner under the command of the twinned forces of the Summer and Winter Courts."

"What's going on," flailed Dogspaw sleepily.

"We've been captured, you idiot," said Starfeather with supreme indifference. "And likely are about to be killed."

61

"We may spare your life, you blubbering piece of offal," I said, "but we demand that you escort us to your leader."

Dogspaw rubbed his eyes. "The Princess!" he cried.

"We wish to negotiate for the release of the prisoner. Should you refuse, your life will be forfeited – and I am sure that Delano would not wish to lose two of his best men..."

"You don't scare us," said Dogspaw with more confidence than perhaps befitted his circumstances. I pressed the blade in deeper into his neck, drawing a small trickle of blood. He relented.

"Fine," he said. "We'll lead you there."

"Get the rope," I said to Shasta, and she scurried to bind both pixies' hands behind their backs. "That will teach you to imprison the friends of the Princess of the Summer Court. Or the Winter Court for that matter. We may be at war, but we will always band together to combat the threat of the Pixies."

"Arise, pig!" cried Shasta, forcing the Pixies to their feet.

The sun had just risen, and the Pixies began to lead us through the forest towards the Pixie Castle I knew all, all too well.

Chapter 5

We spent the day trekking through the forests and glens and glades of Feyland to make it to the Pixie Castle. It was not the distance that took up the time, but the trouble of trying to be led by two pixies who lacked the use of their hands or wings; they stumbled and complained, but we both knew it would be too dangerous to untie them. It was a strange feeling – holding the lives of two creatures in our hands – and when Dogspaw began to complain of an ache in his foot or Starfeather began to bleed from his soles I could not believe my own cruelty in forcing them to carry on. I had always been kind before Feyland – shy, meek – and the idea that I could be in control of these two pixies was at once thrilling and unnerving. I had seen the cold cruelty of the Summer Queen, heard talk of the

Winter Queen. Was I becoming like them, too – so concerned with finding Logan, with winning the war, that I neglected my own basic kindness? Or was I becoming stronger, willing to do what needed to be done in order to achieve my aims?

Shasta had no such compunctions. She whipped the Pixies when they lagged behind and threatened to disembowel them at the slightest provocation. She had been sweet and romantic when the two of us were alone, when she spoke of Rodney, but now it was time for her to behave like a warrior princess – regal, without passion, without regret, without guilt.

We continued onwards towards the bone-like castle – its skeletal towers, its skull-shaped ramparts. It reared up before us like some dead creature floating over the murky waters of its moat; we stared it down, fear rising in our throats like bile.

"Almost there now, Your Highness," said

one of the men, with mocking deference. "Almost at the Castle."

"Carry on then, you foul pig's-breath troll!" said Shasta, concealing her nervousness with another well-aimed insult.

"Not long."

We put our swords to the necks of the Pixies, dragging them roughly as the chain bridge was laid down.

The moment we entered the keep we knew that we had made a mistake. We were outnumbered – pixies swarmed the staircases and the corridors and the courtyards like so many rampant bees – and it would be impossible to outrun them all. We would not be able to make any military advance. And yet the thought of Logan within these towers – so close, still breathing, perhaps still howling in pain from the tortures to which those horrible men had subjected him! - tormented me; my heart stung.

Last time, my only negotiating tactic had

been the promise of marriage to Delano – allying his kingdom with mine in order to save myself from the humiliating fate of being one of Delano's concubines. I steeled myself to breach the subject once more.

"I wish to see the King himself," I said, more bravely than I felt.

"You see him already," said an eerie, high-pitched voice.

I whirled around; Delano was standing behind me.

"I am a Princess," I said. "And you will afford me respect."

He smiled cruelly. "Of course," he said, with a mocking bow that belied his intent. "Two princesses. Two – beautiful – princesses."

"I wish to negotiate for the life of the Wolf," I said.

He laughed. "Negotiate? Two pretty young girls in a den of pixies think they have something to *negotiate* with?" He shrugged. "Kill

Dogspaw and Starfeather if you will. I don't mind."

My dagger tightened around Dogspaw's neck; he had called my bluff. Shasta seemed less bothered – she struck Starfeather heavily with the butt of her sword and he fell to the ground, unconscious but not dead.

"I have something you want," I said, shakily.

"Yes," he said, eyeing me up and down. "Indeed you do. You both do, as a matter of a fact. I know the Winter Fairies cannot bear children – but I am sure I will find...some other use for the dark one."

"You have a choice, my King," I said, with a deep curtsey, echoing his earlier bow. "You could indeed have two concubines."

Shasta whirled on me, her face hot with anger.

"Or," I swallowed deeply. "You can have one wife."

68

Delano had not expected this.

"I wish to speak to you in private," I said. I knew Delano would try to seduce me; I knew I would have to lead him on as long as I could. I, at least, could not stand Shasta seeing me do this. But it was the only way – as long as I cared for Logan, I had to promise myself to him. If I could get out of it later – and I *would,* I willed myself that much – then so much the better. If not – but I couldn't bear to think about the alternative.

"Treat the Princess Shasta with respect," I said. "Or the deal is off."

"You amuse me, Princess," said Delano wryly. "Treat her with the utmost respect, my men." He looked them over. "Or I shall kill each of you personally, tearing out the bones of your neck with my fingers and your vertebrae with my teeth." He looked up at me and it occurred to me that he thought the threat would impress me. As it happened, I only felt rather sick.

He led me into that familiar antechamber where we had once held our audience upon first meeting.

"You wish to marry me?"

I kept my face stony – in a deadpan expression. "I've grown to fall desperately in love with you," I said, my voice dripping with sarcasm.

"I'm not an easy creature to resist, Princess," he said, with equally withering disdain.

"Indeed," I said. "But I can swallow my repulsion. I want the life of the Wolf. I do not love you, nor will I ever. And I will not sign over my kingdom to your control. *However* – however – I wish to destroy the Winter Kingdom as much as you do. And the power of the Pixies allied to one of the Courts, rather than a threat to both, is a shrewd political move. My people have grown to hate their fairy kin in the Winter lands, far more even than they hate the Pixies who threaten their borders with border raids and banditry. A marriage to you would help me defeat the Winter Court and stop the Pixie raids on fairy people – beneficial to me. And I would bear us the strongest sons in the land." This part sickened me. "Beneficial to you."

"In many ways, Princess," he said. He was impressed; I could see it in his eyes. "But that is not why you wish to marry me, is it?"

"It's not your beauty," I said hotly, and I could see that beneath his regal hauteur Delano was stung. He was not monstrous, to be sure – but his face had the eerie glow of decadence, of dissipation. It was not a human face; it was too cruel for that. "I love Logan," I said, and the moment I said it I knew it was true. I did not love him the way I loved Kian – with that mad, passionate longing that came only out of magic – but I trusted him; I felt bound to him. I had known Kian for weeks; I had loved Logan all of my life. "And I am willing to take whatever measures necessary. I ask also that you allow me to return Shasta home. We may well destroy the Winter Court yet," I said, "but we will do so under fairy rules of honor – not pixie laws of chaos."

"You judge me harshly, Princess," said Delano. "You fairies have taken the land that belongs by birthright to us pixies. We conduct border raids on you, our oppressors. We are the lone rebels of the ancient creatures who existed here before you fairies took over – with your harmony, your geometry, your laws. Our magic is not your magic. It is darker, more mysterious. We believe in love, in the arts of the bedroom – yes, Princess, I see you blush, but *our* pixies are fertile – and yes, in pain, in death. We *feel* the way you fairies do not feel." He drew himself up and I could see pride flashing across his face, replacing his cruelty. "So do not accuse pixies of chaos. We own this land. It is ours by right! You, my dear princess, are the invader – not us!"

I let my eyes fall to the floor. "What do I care?" I said at last, giving way to anger. "Whether this land belongs to pixies – to fairies? Summer or Winter or pixie or fairy – well, Delano, *Your Highness*, I don't give a damn!"

He looked surprised.

"I grew up as a child in the Land Beyond the Crystal River. I had a mother, and I had friends – friends like Logan, whom you have captured. I have no part in these wars. I want no part in these wars. I do not want to bear your children – or anyone else's – I'm *sixteen*, and where I come from that makes me a child and you a pervert! So don't you blame me for this! I don't care if you're a pixie or a fairy – I'm not kindly disposed towards anyone who wants to hurt or imprison those I care about. I just want to go home!"

Tears stung my eyes; I tried to blink them back and act like a princess.

But something I had said had struck

Delano. I saw in his face a new expression – something I had never seen before! His anger and pride had gone; instead he only looked abashed, surprised. In his eyes I saw something not unlike compassion – something not unlike humanity.

"Very well," he said quietly. "I shall think this over. I will have a servant direct you to an antechamber. I need to think."

"Delano," I said softly. His change in demeanor had surprised me.

"I need to think!" he repeated, shouting louder. "Now get out of here before I decide to have you executed."

He took one last look at me and then stormed off to the window, staring out at the storm gathering around the castle.

I gave him a deep curtsey, my face red with shock, before the guard escorted me out.

Chapter 6

The next morning, I was awakened before dawn by the crude rapping of one of the guards at my door, his fists pounding sharply against the wood. I murmured aloud softly, covering my head with a pillow. It was, despite the imprisonment, the most comfortable bed I had been given during my time in Feyland, and in the semi somnolent stirrings of morning I had forgotten where I was. I thought that I was back in Gregory, Oregon, my mother pounding on the door to remind me that I was late for school. I curled into a little ball, willing away the noise. Just five more minutes, I thought to myself – and then I'd force myself to get up, to pack my backpack. I wanted to lose myself in the dreamy oblivion of sleep for a few moments longer.

The knock came again, louder this time. "Princess!" came a voice. "The Pixie King

75

demands an audience with you immediately."

Princess. Pixie king. The words were like gunpowder blasts, sparking me into thought and action. I remembered who and where I was. Pain gripped at my heart as I rose. "One moment..." I called. "Let me get dressed!"

I went to the wardrobe, but found that the simple fairy dress the Summer Queen had supplied me with was gone. In its place was a long gown of flowing green silk, dotted with tiny emeralds along the neckline and the helm. It was pixie craft – I recognized the unmistakable marks of cruel magic in the tightness of the seams, the flowing light in and out of the emeralds. When I put on the dress I felt the fabric suck inside itself, molding itself to the contours of my body. I looked beautiful, I thought, as I gazed upon my reflection in the mirror. But it was a cold beauty, eerie and unearthly; I was not comfortable in my own skin.

"Princess!" The knock came a final time.

I emerged from the bedroom.

"I'm ready," I said quietly.

The guards led me down the long, glimmering corridor. I gulped as I saw the decorations – the skulls and skeletons hanging up by chains along the wet stones. If this was pixie art, I thought, I was perfectly happy in a room far less decorated. But I had to be strong, to be brave. Logan was in this castle, I thought – nearby. He could even perhaps hear my footsteps; would he be comforted by them? I concentrated on my magic and tried to connect with Logan, to use my magic to hear his voice, to see him.

Logan, I whispered, in that sacred cloister of myself from which magic came. *Please, Logan, are you there?*

In a flash, I saw him, in my mind's eye but as clear as if he were right before me. And yet I did not see him – I *felt* him, became as aware of him and of his surroundings as if my soul had been transported into his body; I felt his sorrow, felt his worry, felt his pain.

I felt a howl call out from my throat, a howl of sorrow and agony.

"*I will not go,*" Logan was crying out. "*I will not leave her!*"

I heard his thoughts rippling beneath the surface. *Breena – Breena, my love.*

I could not breathe. Vaguely I was aware that I was still being led down the corridor by the guards; I had to keep walking. And yet all my attention was fixed on Logan, in pain now, but not the physical torment the Pixies had enacted upon him earlier. No, this was the pain of love, a pain I could well understand, to which I could well relate.

"*She will not marry you!*" Logan was shouting at Delano, his voice and face contorted in snarls of hatred. "*I will not go! Kill me if you must! Murder me, torture me, roast me alive! She must not marry you! She does not love you!"*

Did I love Logan? I couldn't tell. My heart was so full of his love for me; our telepathic link had brought love firmly into my soul, and I could not separate out what I felt for him from what he felt for me.

"You are being selfish," said Delano. *"You see – it is not merely your life or your happiness at stake, nor Breena's. The Princess Shasta is here – and I will allow her to go free only if you consent to leave – if Breena consents to marry me. If you do anything to thwart my plans, this innocent woman's life will be forfeited."*

I could feel Logan's raging stop, his lupine wrath restrained as his human compassion took over. No, as hurt and angry and scared as Logan was, he would never allow an innocent to suffer. He had risked his life to save Kian, who was far from innocent; he would never allow Shasta to be sacrificed.

"Very well," said Logan, his voice tight as a

coiled spring. *"But let me see her first. Breena – let me see her."*

My heart leaped! I wanted nothing more than to see Logan again, to wrap my arms around him, to smell that familiar musk on his neck and clothes that always reminded me of the woods, of the great expanses of nature where in happier days we had been allowed to wander unrestrained and to be ourselves – free of mortal dithering and fairy politics alike. I missed those woods. I missed Logan.

"Not until I have married her," said Delano. *"The last thing I want is for a young strapping brute like youself to sniff around the Princess, changing her mind. I cannot force her marriage. I will allow you to return to visit her, and to kiss her feet and offer your Queen thanks for your miserable life, once I have secured her promise of marriage. Halfling,"* and here Delano looked down disgusted, *"marriage is not like in your filthy mortal world – a mere exchange of words.*

Marriage is binding, here – magic of two fused into one."

"What will you do to me?" Logan asked, his face steely with bravery.

"Let you go," Delano shrugged. *"I am an honorable pixie, after all. And when Breena sees you have gone, she will have no choice but to uphold her word. After all, I still have the Princess Shasta – as insurance..."*

"Honorable!" Logan spat. *"Is that what you call making a woman who doesn't love you marry you?"*

"Perfectly honorable. I did not have to let you go. You are fairly our prisoner – you killed several of my men. And she is fairly agreeing to an exchange...fair's fair. But I wouldn't expect a filthy animal like you to understand justice!"

And with that my connection with Logan was broken, as I was led into the antechamber once more.

"Sit," barked the guards. "Sit down, girl!"

"Princess," muttered another guard, wilier in the ways of diplomacy.

"Fine, Princess then," said the first one. And they left me to wait until at last Delano appeared from behind what seemed to be a secret passageway.

"Come with me, Princess," said Delano, his voice smooth and silky.

He took my hand; I shuddered. Could I stand to let this creature touch me every night? I had to find a way out – *some way out...*

"I have let your Wolf-boy go," said Delano. "Look out the window."

I saw, in the distance, a troop of pixie guards escorting Logan into the snowy banks of the mountain base. When a trumpet was sounded, they threw him into the snow and marched back into formation, heading back towards the castle, leaving Logan alone – wounded, but alive. I saw him stagger up; instinctively I leaned forward, out the window, ready to shout...

"He won't hear you," said Delano. "Look how far away he is."

"And Shasta?"

"Shasta is well. I won't release her – not yet. Not until the ceremony is finalized. It can be your first order as Pixie Queen – the order to release her."

"Is she being kept under good conditions? I want to see where she is being kept!"

"In a state room like yours, Princess. Fear not. You are a good negotiator; I admire that in a woman. I will not break my word. It costs me nothing to be kind to her. Only the price of a few bolts of pixie silk. I got her a dress too, you see." He fingered the folds of the dress he had given me. "You see, even if I am to let her go...untouched." he sneered. "I should at least get the pleasure of looking at a woman at her best."

"You're digusting!" I moved away from

him. "I'm sixteen!"

"Well of age in Feyland," said Delano. "And you're mortal – at that. You will die soon."

"Soon?"

"In a hundred years you will be dead." Delano shrugged. "Moments, for a pixie. Just moments. And every second that passes you get older, your beauty closer to fading away. I don't see the point of waiting. You, my dearest Princess, are almost dead already – in terms of how we pixies view time. You are like a delicate hothouse flower, destined to bloom only for a short while."

I felt sick.

"You are beautiful – you are fertile. And your ephemeral mortality only makes you that much more desirable. I don't want to waste any time in experiencing you."

"That's disgusting!" I said.

"What, sex?" He said it with a shrug. "For humans, perhaps. For fairies – certainly! They are the most prudish of all the races. But not for pixies. We are like your animals – no regret, no fear, no hesitations. We let our instincts run free. We see nothing shameful about desire."

He saw my cheeks blush; he stroked them lightly. "But you do."

"Where I come from, you'd be arrested!" I said, my voice shaking.

"Where I come from, you'd be married already," he said, and shrugged again. "Do not apply your human standards to me."

I couldn't help it; tears began trickling down my eyes. I tried to think of Logan – connect with him again – feel where he was, see what he saw...

In my mind's eye I saw a Wolf, prowling through the snow, his eyes hot with rage and pain. And I saw a knight approaching him – a knight in the familiar garb of the Summer Court, with kind eyes and a soft smile and long, red hair that shone in the wintry breezes. I knew him – my instincts took over – he was one of my men, of my court. He was a man I had heard described many times before.

Rodney.

Chapter 7

Later that day Delano summoned me to his room again. He had left out another dress for me in the wardrobe – a deep, scarlet blood-red that clung around my waist and my chest, accentuating features I had never before been aware that I had. I did not like it. I looked too old, too alluring – like a woman of twenty-five or thirty. I was only sixteen, and although I had wished plenty of times back at Gregory High School for my hair to grow lighter, my breasts to grow just a bit larger, my waist to narrow further, I now wished for all the world that I could be back in my plain T-shirts and torn jeans at Gregory High, wandering through the woods with Logan without any care more pressing than fourth period math or the potential destruction of the woods behind

87

Gregory High School. But I allowed myself to slip the dress over my head, felt the tightening of the embroidery around me, and gazed at myself mournfully in the mirror before allowing Delano to take me away.

He met me in the ante-chamber.

"Not here," said Delano. "I want to show you something." He took hold of my hand, his icy skin causing my own to shiver, and led me through the ante-chamber into a hidden room at the back.

It looked nothing like the chamber. While his throne room was cold and dank – a place to inspire fear and even pain in his audience – this was a room to be lived in. There was a bed in the corner – a luxurious four-poster canopy bed with heavy black silken sheets hanging down from it. The tapestries covered the cold stone of the castle, giving a sense of warmth to the room I had not seen elsewhere in my stay among the Pixies. And there was a roaring, magical fire in the fireplace – glinting yellow and red, green and black in turn – casting a warm light upon us both.

Against myself, I sighed. I had not realized how cold I had been for the past twenty-four hours until the wonderful warmth of the fireplace lapped up against me. I forgot my decorum and my fear and rushed over to the fireplace, letting the prickling warmth of the hearth surround me.

I looked up at Delano; he was smiling. It was a kinder smile than I had seen him sport in time past.

"See, we Pixies are not all bad," he said. "If you are to marry me, you will be treated kindly – like a Queen. I am not a monster."

"You're not a monster," I conceded. "But you are cruel."

"Perhaps," Delano gave me a grim sigh. "But my cruelty has prevented you fairies from easily taking over my land. The fear Summer and Winter share alike of me has kept my kingdom going. And I am not averse to being cruel." He came over to me and caressed my cheek. "But I can also be kind. And I will be kind to you, Breena."

I shuddered away from his touch; Delano stared at me, abashed. It had not truly occurred to him that any princess could avoid his seductions for long. Perhaps he thought me so terrified of him in his crueler state that this little kindness would make me fall for him. Instead, I was only more disgusted than ever. He wasn't being kind for the sake of it. He was trying to seduce me!

"I would rather you be neither kind nor cruel," I said harshly, "but only fair and practical. If I am to marry you – I won't pretend I'm in love with you. I will bear you children if and when you require it but I want my independence. I want to live in the Summer Court – or at least be permitted to visit – and to spend as much time away from you as possible." I threw my hair back. "Don't pretend I'll love you."

Delano almost looked hurt. "Very well," he said. "No pretending."

He took my hand and pressed it to his lips; I drew it away and slapped him. "Don't try it, Delano," I said.

He pressed his hand to his cheek, where a red, welt-like bruise was spreading over his pallid skin. "How dare you?" he spat. "How dare you defy me?"

"You want to marry me," I shouted, roused at last to full-fledged rage. "Fine! Marry me! But I won't make it easy or pleasant for you." I looked straight into his eyes, my own flashing with anger. "Don't expect any love from me."

I turned around and stormed out, leaving Delano standing agape, his mouth wide with shock and hurt.

Let him be hurt, I thought. I didn't care.

In his rage Delano had neglected to summon the guards, or to call them to attention, so I wandered the corridors of the castle alone. It was the first time in days I had been allowed to wander where I wanted – nobody's prisoner, at least for the moment. I stormed down the sides and corridors of the castle, up and down staircases, through rooms and portrait galleries – all empty. The guards, presumably, were kept down in the courtyard; Delano liked his privacy up here.

Suddenly I felt a hand clamp over my mouth.

"Don't scream," came a whispered voice. It was not frightening; there was something calming and soft in it. "My name is Rodney," said the voice. "I am a loyal subject and a knight of the Summer Court. I am here to free you."

I nodded; he let me go.

"How did you..." I began.

"We swam," said Rodney, shaking out

some wet hair onto the ground. "Enchanted the dolphins in the moat so they could communicate with us – tell us a good way in."

"We?"

"Logan is here too – he's gone to get the Princess Shasta." When Rodney spoke her name, his love for her was clear; I could see in the darkness how the blush had spread like a rose bloom over his cheeks. "We have a secret passageway out. I think it's been in disuse for a while – probably originally for spies to get out unnoticed during the Fairy Siege."

"Fairy Siege?"

"We've tried to conquer the Pixies many times," said Rodney with nonchalance. "But never have we succeeded."

I thought of Delano's rage – calling me, calling us the oppressors – but said nothing.

"Quick, it's this way – we can do it stealthily. Enchant your footsteps, if you can. Make sure nobody can hear or see you."

Rodney took hold of my hand and led me through one of the portrait galleries – a whole host of pixie kings frozen in time like insects in amber.

When we arrived at the entrance to the passageway, secreted behind a portrait of King Pranzide the Second, we saw a blue ribbon tied around one of the protruding stones.

"It's a sign!" said Rodney. "Shasta and Logan have already made it out. Let's go."

My heart began thumping loudly. The promise of seeing Logan again, of being close to him and feeling his arms wrapped tightly around me, was almost more than I could bear. But I had to stay strong. I had to get out alive.

My hand wrapped tightly in Rodney's, I stumbled down the long passageway – spiral stairs after spiral stairs, that led down to an entrance to the moat.

"Now," said Rodney. "Hold your breath. And swim!"

Forever Frost (Bitter Frost Series #2)

We plunged together into the dark waters. I felt something slimy touch me and started; in terror I opened my eyes and felt relief slacken my muscles. It was a dolphin, sleek and noble, with its fins protruding out towards me. Rodney nudged me, creating a stream of bubbles in the water, and I seized hold of one of the flippers; Rodney took the other. In a flash of jetsam the dolphin took off, propelling out from the moat, taking us to the other side of the bank...

My heart was pounding harder now, and I couldn't breathe; I felt my fingers loosen on the dolphin's flippers, my mind blank in and out of consciousness...

At last we reached the shore. Rodney helped me scramble up to the side of the bank and we looked up together at the dark castle above us – impenetrable at first, with so many secret ways in and out...

"You have done well, Master Dolphin," whispered Rodney, patting the creature on the head. "When the Fairies reconquer the Pixie lands – you shall be made a knight of the Navy!"

The dolphin bubbled out a joyous assent.

"Rodney!" I heard Shasta's whisper break the spell of night.

"Bree!" And it was a voice I knew all too well.

Shasta and Logan appeared on the horizon.

Overjoyed, we rushed towards them.

Chapter 8

Before we had time to properly engage with each other or with our surroundings, Rodney led us deep into the night-black forests, the underbrush clinging to our feet. We were all too excited, our hearts beating too quickly, to take in what was going on; Rodney, at least, had the presence of mind to steer us into where we wouldn't be caught.

"Light an invisibility circle," he whispered hoarsely, and Shasta and I began the same low, soft chant that she had first taught me upon first making our escape, concentrating our magic on securing the borders of our campsite between two stretching fir trees.

"We made it," whispered Shasta at last, when we had at last created for ourselves a little campsite of safety. "We made it." Her whisper turned into a joyous shout; her face – ecstatic, radiant – was even more luminous than usual in the flickering of the magical candles we had lit on each tiny needle of the fir tree. "Oh, Rodney."

Decorum forgotten, the two of them threw themselves into each other's arms, wrapping themselves so tightly around each other than in the shadows they seemed less like two fairies in love than like a single, dynamic being, so full of life and love and energy that a thousand mortal bodies could not have contained it.

"I missed you so much, Rodney," whispered Shasta. "And I didn't even get to say goodbye – when I had to go away....I had to go home – but I even tried to run back! But I couldn't – not with so many lives at stake...so much at stake..." She was no longer the regal princess now; now, as Rodney stroked her hair and softly cupped her face in his hands, she was as girlish and sweet as any mortal.

"I understand," said Rodney. "It would

have been too dangerous for you to come back. But that's why I went – you see – I followed you both! I would have offered myself up as a prisoner in the Winter Court and then you could have been my captor – my jailer! Already you have the key to my heart."

Logan gave an uncomfortable cough and shuffle of his feet. Against the overwhelming passion of Shasta and Rodney, my own reunion with Logan seemed clumsy – awkward – unsure. It was so easy for them to vanish into their whirlwind of emotions, to forget that we were watching them as they covered each other's faces and hands and mouths with kisses.

"We can't be apart ever again," I heard Rodney saying as he kissed Shasta's neck. I was grateful for the dim flickering of the lights; I was blushing a shade of scarlet more suited to shades of fruit than shades of complexion, and I didn't want Logan to see how uncomfortable all this was making me. I could tell that he felt awkward too; he was standing stiffly at a distance.

"Logan..." I tried to say. I tried to greet him, tried to explain – explain how sorry I was, how much I'd missed him, how I wasn't sure – and yet I knew that when I thought he was dead my whole world had collapsed and inverted upon itself. There was so much to say and yet I couldn't for all my magic find a way of saying it, of expressing it. And I was afraid, too, of what Logan had to say to me. Would there be anger? Would he reproach me? Would he...

And then I didn't have time to think any longer. I saw Logan set his jaw with firm resolve and turn towards me. In a few striding steps he was in front of me, his face close to mine, and then his hands were on my shoulders, pulling me towards him, pulling my mouth towards his.

And then he kissed me.

In the brief seconds between the time he began walking towards me and the time when our lips were finally, finally touching, I had a series of thoughts. I thought of resisting, of apologizing; I thought of Kian, of that magical and terrifying week in his hunting-lodge in the Winter badlands, of my dreams of fairy waltzes, of my fear, my apologies, my anger at myself, how overwhelmed I was by Feyland and pixies and marriage and politics and war – always war! And yet when Logan's lips were on mine, bruising my mouth with the full intensity of his passion, none of these things seemed to matter to me. His arms were locked around the back of my neck, pressing me towards him with the full animal force of him – his kisses had in them the strength and vigor of a wolf! I felt my knees going weak; I felt my mouth opening up to his.

It was not like my first kiss with Kian. That had been as delicately dangerous as shattered glass – a beautiful, magical moment as still and picturesque as one of Kian's fairy paintings on the walls of his hunting-lodge. It had been like a dream – a gorgeous, wonderful dream but a dream nonetheless. This felt real. I could smell the familiar musk on his neck and his chest. I could taste his lips, feel the bristle of the stubble on his chin. This was the Logan I had almost kissed on my birthday, before the Pixie King came, before Kian came and I was dragged into Feyland and changed forever. This was my best friend – the person to whom I had confided all my secrets, all my fears and worries, for ten years or more. His kiss was not new or strange; rather, it was familiar – containing all the friendship and love and trust that had passed between us in the ten years of our friendship.

At last he pulled away, kissing my forehead and my hand.

"Let's talk," he said, his voice low and soft as he led me behind a great oak tree – as much to give Shasta and Rodney privacy as to make sure we were not heard.

"I missed you," I said, my voice shaking. "And – Logan – I'm so sorry..."

"You've risked your life at the Pixie Castle twice now," said Logan, ruffling my hair. "First for Kian, then for me. Breena, you're the bravest girl I know."

"I missed you," I said, snuggling down into his chest. "So much. I didn't know until I thought you were dead – how much I felt...how strongly..."

He stroked my hair. "I never told you," he said. "I was a coward. It was only when I let some... fairy prince almost steal your heart that I realized I had to tell you – or risk losing you. And then it was too late – and you seemed so happy..."

"I don't want to live without you in my life," I said. "When I thought you were dead, it was like something huge and empty opened up inside me; I couldn't stand it! I would have done anything – even married Delano – to get you back..."

"I'm glad you didn't," he said, hugging me tightly.

"My mother," I broke in. "She's at the Winter Court. That's why..."

"Rodney explained it to me," said Logan, grinning. "He's a nice guy, Rodney. Although I do hope Summer-Winter couplings don't become the fashion in Feyland."

I blushed; I didn't want him to remind me of Kian. I knew he was jealous, but I could not stand to speak ill of Kian, whom I had not seen since my abduction at the hands of the Summer Court.

"So, what now?" I asked.

"Well, let's start by getting your mother out of Feyland. As far as I recall your mother liked the beach, not the cold – I imagine she's not enjoying her vacation at the Winter Court." Logan chuckled. "I'm sure she's fine – they don't mistreat hostages there."

"But the Summer Court says..."

"The Winter Court says your Queen roasts hostages alive. As far as I can tell, Shasta hasn't been roasted anytime lately."

He had a point.

"And then what?" I asked Logan, leaning my head on his shoulder.

"And then," said Logan, giving me an affectionate tap on the nose, "I say you, me, and your mother head back beyond the Crystal River, and return to normal."

Normal. The word filled me at once with joy and dread. I wanted to be safe, to sleep, to be with those I loved without worrying about other people's wars, other people's magic. And yet – could I bear to leave Feyland?

"I'll make sure you all get to Gregory safely," said Logan, kissing my forehead again.

It was then that we heard the sharp sound of rustling among the leaves. Wary of a pixie attack, we jumped up, looking back around

105

behind the tree.

We heard the crunch of leaves, of footsteps – two pairs of footsteps, running off into the distance.

Shasta and Rodney had gone.

Chapter 9

Immediately we sprang into action, scanning the dark clearings, the shadowy pathways, for any sign of Rodney or Shasta. Had the Pixies taken them? No – we reasoned – there was no way any pixie could have crossed the magical threshold that we had created together with our spell. The only way the perimeter could have been broken was if Shasta and Rodney had left on their own accord...

"Run!" Logan shouted at me, and together we dashed, hand in hand, through the leafy night, following the sounds – growing faster and faster now – of footsteps crunching leaves ahead of us. We ran and the wind whipped our faces and our hair; I could feel Logan's hand grow more powerful, furrier, as he began to transition into the Wolf form.

"Get on my back," he roared, his voice changing from human scream to lupine howl, and I assented, gripping his flowing hair between my fingers and feeling the power of his muscles ripple beneath my legs.

As a wolf, Logan was faster than any fairy, and soon we were able to gain on them, seeing their figures ever more clearly in the distance. They were running away! Shasta and Rodney, hands locked together, almost out of breath now, running away from us....

"Stop!" I called out to them, my voice by now exhausted from the run. "Stop!"

We caught up with them near a ravine, where a precipitous drop seemed a less palatable option for the two of them than stopping to face us directly. They stopped short, their feet dragging briefly in the earth, and then turned to face us.

Suddenly, we felt a blinding green flash envelop us, strike us, knock us back! Rodney and Shasta had used their magic on us! I felt something wet trickle down my cheek and knew that it must be blood; anger boiled up in me! Had we not just helped Shasta escape from the Pixie Court! And now she was trying to run away again!

"Stop!" I cried again, tasting blood in my mouth. I focused my anger inwardly – I need to stop them, to bind them, just to hold them still a little longer....

A blue flash counteracted their green one, and both Rodney and Shasta stumbled back.

"Don't take me home!" cried Shasta, her voice hot with rage. "I'm in love, Bree! Don't try to stop me!"

She sent another blast of magical anger our way.

"Try to stop you from destroying innocent lives and running away, you mean?"

"Rodney and I will be separated if you make us go home!" she yelled back. "Well, I won't do it! I refuse to do it!"

I struck her once more with my magic, and now I could see a spot of blood gathering at the side of her lips.

I slid off Logan's back and began heading towards them; behind me, I could hear a rush of sound as Logan started transforming from beast back into man.

"You can't make me go back there!" shouted Shasta, with all the inchoate brattiness of a teenage girl. "You can't make me."

"Like hell I can't," I muttered to myself, trying to cast a binding spell. But Shasta was almost as strong as I was – perhaps even stronger – and she continued to resist the nebulous smoky chains that were beginning to materialize around her and Rodney's legs and arms, brought into being by my magic...

"I don't want to go home!"

"Stop!" cried a booming, powerful voice. It was Logan, striding towards the two of them, letting their attack-magic bounce off him, ignoring the pain that every blast must surely have inflicted upon him. "Stop it right now!"

"Please," moaned Shasta. "Just go away and let us be. Beyond the Crystal River."

"And sacrifice Breena's mother?" Logan roared, and I could still hear the Wolf in his voice.

"And sacrifice Breena? And what about all the innocent fairy lives that will be taken if the war drags on? Are they worth your emotions?"

"I don't care," said Shasta stubbornly, but her voice was shaking. "I just want to be with Rodney."

Rodney looked at the ground, ashamed. He knew what Logan was saying was true.

"You can't just run away from your problems, Princess," he said. "I know we'd all like to sometimes. But there are more important things than love. Like bravery – and honor. Like doing right by your friends. Like doing right by your country. By the people who trust you to lead them. You could be a Queen one day, Shasta; act like it!"

"Spoken like a true fairy," Rodney muttered. Werewolves were not looked upon with much respect in Feyland; this was a great compliment indeed.

Rodney gently laid down his sword at our feet. Shasta bit her lip, staring us down a moment longer, before she too nodded and lay down her weapon.

"And perhaps the Winter Queen will show you some mercy yet," said Logan. "She is a mother, after all. Beneath the Queen there is a mother, too."

"If only," said Shasta softly. "My mother doesn't care if I'm happy or not – as long as I make her proud."

"Your country is at war," said Logan, with uncompromising harshness in his voice – he almost sounded like Kian, I thought. "Your happiness is less important than the lives of your people."

"And peace would bring us both!" Shasta cried.

For that was the truth. Beyond our talk of sacrifice and duty, beyond our talk of love, the truth was that peace between our two kingdoms would do more for both our happiness and that of the citizens of the Fairy Kingdoms than any battle or act of heroism could do.

"Then let us bring peace," said Logan, at last smiling. He offered her his hand; at last she took it. "Let us bring peace between the Kingdoms – *stay* in Feyland and work towards these noble ends, rather than running away and leaving our country torn in war."

"I have behaved dishonorably, Wolf," said Rodney. "For this I am sorry. I have behaved in a manner unfitting a knight of the Fairy Court." He was careful not to specify which Fairy Court. He turned to Shasta. "My lady," he said, kneeling to kiss her hand. "You are a fool to love one so selfish and dishonorable as I."

"And you, my knight," she said, her diction of these chivalric formulae pitch-perfect, "are unwise to love one so selfish and dishonorable as I." She turned back towards me. "We have not behaved fittingly. We have behaved like children." Now calmed down, she was careful to speak in the rich melodies and precise diction of a princess, rather than the babbling incoherencies of a teenaged girl. "I apologize; we lay ourselves at your feet and at your mercy."

"Well, there's no need for that," I said, a bit taken aback. "Just promise you won't do it again."

"We swear a sacred oath," said Shasta. "We will not run away again. We swear by the ancient laws and the old codes."

"So we swear," echoed Rodney. They both nodded, as if to confirm it to the heavens.

"Right," said Logan. "It's nearly dawn,

114

now. Should we head back? Maybe have some breakfast? Sweep all of this under the rug."

It was difficult to stay angry with Shasta and Rodney. They had only done, in the end, what Kian and I had so longed to do. (Kian! But I couldn't think of that now.)

We returned to our campsite, and once more Shasta and I repeated the magical incantation that secured our borders against invasion. We lit a fire and Rodney brought out some fruits and meats from his pouch, which we attempted to roast over the open flame, speared by twigs and branches.

Shasta nuzzled up to me. "Who is he?" she asked. "Your Wolf? Have you forgotten my brother so quickly?"

It was a question I knew I had to answer sooner or later. "Your brother," I said, "I care for very deeply. But I cannot allow myself to think of him. You are not the Crown Princess – your love is perhaps possible. I cannot think of it." It was mostly true – I had neglected to mention my conflicted feelings towards Logan, how unsure I was of myself – if I saw them both before me now, both in love with me, both wanting me, I still had no idea which of them I would choose.

"The Wolf and I have known each other for ten years – ten human years. And I value his counsel highly." I sounded like a princess, I thought. Just like her.

"Is that all you value?" whispered Shasta to me. I felt my face flush once more with shame. Was I doing the right thing? I didn't know. All I knew is that I wanted to feel Logan's arms around me once more, that familiar musk at his neck, the softness of his lips.

Logan came over to me and took my hand, enveloping it in his; absent-mindedly, I stroked his hand, his wrist, ruffled his hair. He placed his arms around me in a great bear hug, pressing me deep into his chest. He was warm; he was safe. I closed my eyes and felt the glimmering flame from the campfire prickle comfortably against my skin. I wanted to stay like this – far from pixies, far from fairies, far from war – with a boy I loved, and who I knew to love me.

"I shall cook," said Rodney, with a slight bow. "A feast to express my apologies for troubling the two of you. Logan – would you help me?"

"Gladly," said Logan. "I love to cook." He smiled sadly and I knew he was looking at me, thinking of me, thinking of the last time we cooked together. It was my birthday, and he had come over to surprise me, and we had together made tortilla chips and all manner of dishes and filled the house with flour powder as we laughingly chased each other up and downstairs, carefree. It was my sixteenth birthday, and hours later Delano had arrived, and then Kian had come, and then all else after that seemed so strange to me that it did not seem to belong to the same world at all, but rather to a whole other existence, a whole other girl.

He had nearly kissed me then. As he looked at me, his great brown eyes crinkling ever so slightly at the corners, I knew he was remembering that prelude to our kiss – the way he had leaned so close to me...the way I had leaned back...

I knew he was wondering the same thing that I had wondered many times. If he had been a second sooner, if Delano had been a second later. If his lips had touched mine – if I had opened my lips to his and let him kiss me with all the passion that had been building up inside him for ten years – then would I have been so taken with Kian, the boy I danced the Fairy Waltz with while a toddler in Feyland? Would I have been so ready to fall for him? I was sixteen – I had never been kissed – I had dreamed of romance so often and yet I had never been kissed, never known any more about love than what I had read in fairy-tales and fantasy novels. All these feelings were overwhelming to me – the way I could be so passionate about Kian one minute and then so in love with Logan the next – the way my emotions could tumble over themselves like snowballs in an avalanche, beyond my control, beyond my power.

When I was fifteen I remembered thinking that I was so grown up, so above the petty confidences and insecurities growing like moss in the locker room of Gregory High School. Ever since I had turned sixteen, I had started feeling younger than ever – or at least that the world was so much bigger, so full of feeling and passion and contradiction that I could barely make myself out, let alone the identity of my beloved.

Hormones, my mother would have said.

"Logan," I whispered.

"What is it, Bree?" He had by now finished

preparing the roast, and had ceded the job of cooking it properly to Rodney, who was working extra hard to make up for his unchivalrous acts earlier.

"I don't want you to be in danger again," I said. "I want you to go home with my mother to Gregory – and stay out of trouble."

"I don't mind trouble," said Logan. "I mind being away from you."

"Please..." I said. And I knew what I had to say; I looked up. "I don't want to feel responsible for you. And..." This part was harder to say. "I don't want to feel like...this is all moving so fast..."

I thought I loved him, but I didn't want to force myself to be sure just yet. And if Logan risked his life for me again, I didn't want this to bind me to him romantically. I couldn't ask him to take risks for me out of love, when my own feelings were so nebulous, so confused. I didn't want to lie to him.

"You don't have to rescue me," I concluded miserably, trying to find a way to give voice to my feelings. "I care for you – as a friend – so much – and as more...I think....but this is happening so fast. And I don't want you to feel obligated – *I* don't want to feel..."

"Obligated?" said Logan, cutting me off with just a hint of bitterness. He sighed deeply. "Bree – I'm not that kind of guy. If I do risk my life for you – it's because I care about you, because I believe in you. Not because I want anything in return. Even if you didn't feel anything for me – as hard as that would be for me, I'd still be here beside you, risking my life for you, fighting for you."

He cupped his face with my hand.

"I do feel things for you," I said. "But I don't want to start something in a situation like this...not fully...not yet..."

"I understand," said Logan.

"And I can't let you get tortured because of

me again!"

"I'd do it all over again," said Logan. "And not because you kissed me afterward – although it was so – so – worth it. But because I love you. You don't even know how much. And I would go to the ends of the Earth for you, Bree."

His words warmed me; his words scared me. I was overcome by the beauty of his love; at the same time, I was wary of it. How could I feel the same way about him – or about Kian – or about anyone else, for that matter – when I was still trying to figure out how to get to the Winter Court without being waylaid by pixies or kewpies or any other creature out of *Causabon's Mythology.*

"Thank you, Logan," I said. I pressed his hand to mine and realized that it was wet with tears – both mine and his. He knew me so well – it touched me so deeply that my soul felt as if it were being torn open, rent apart by this storm of feelings. "It means a lot to me."

Forever Frost (Bitter Frost Series #2)

Logan squeezed my hand. "I am so grateful for the chance to get to know you," he said. "You were the one thing that made the Land Beyond the Crystal River bearable to me. When I had to go back and forth...I always looked forward to seeing you."

He kissed my forehead.

"Let's keep things...let's take them slow for now," I said, breathing deeply. "I don't want to rush anything."

"I won't rush you," said Logan, and his voice contained so much love, so much passion, so much pain, that the tears came faster from me, now. He knew me so well, I thought; he knew me better than I knew myself. He was loving; he was giving me space and time to figure out what I was feeling, what was going on.

We caught sight of Shasta and Rodney in the moonlight. They were sitting by the campfire, kissing passionately as if there were no cares for each other but each other; they were in love, they were happy. Everything was so easy for them, I thought. Yes – there were the differences and difficulties borne out of their opposing factions, but that was circumstance. Summer or Winter, they knew how they felt; they knew what they wanted. Everything was so straightforward for them. But for us it was complicated; for us it was harder. My feelings were a tangle of complications.

How could I bring Logan into this? How could I bring myself into this?

I curled up after our meal and waited for day to come properly, to allow us to set off on our way. I waited for my mother, my family, my life to begin anew. I waited for deliverance; the hours seemed endless.

Chapter 10

It took us another two days of travel to reach the Winter Court. Had we gone in a straight line, going as quickly as possible, it should only have taken us about a day, but the four of us were careful. We knew we had Pixies on our trail, and Feyland was filled with other dangers as well. We were wary of bandits, of kewpies that could be lying in wait for us, or of rogue fairy knights from either side looking to score bounty. Could this be the same land I dreamed about in my childhood, I wondered? The Feyland of which I had so often dreamed for sixteen years had been a beautiful place – of great awe and great magic – but it had not been so perilous, so filled with evil. This land had been broken, I realized, battered and ravaged by war. The Pixies had gained power in the absence of a clear fairy leader. Lawlessness raged all around us. And so Rodney, Logan, Shasta and I had to travel with great care, casting magic glamours to conceal us from any potential enemies, traveling at night and sleeping during the day, always with one of us keeping watch in case the Pixies should be able to pass beyond the boundaries of the magical perimeter we had created for safety. Rodney and Shasta slept next to each other, tangled and twisted with immeasurable passion in each other's arms. But Logan and I had more trouble trying to figure out what to do. I was sure that I wanted to take things slowly, carefully; I didn't want to rush into anything. And yet no matter how far apart we placed our mattresses, no matter how much space we left between us as we settled down, I found that I always woke up curled into his arms, my body and soul drawn towards him as we slept, towards his warmth, his protective arms.

When we woke up, we'd blush and sigh

and try to keep our tenuous friendship – knowing all the while how we felt about each other – but I could not deny the beauty of waking up in Logan's arms, feeling his heart beat against my cheek, and feeling the rhythms of my heart move to match his.

At last on the third day of travel we reached the Winter Court. It was an awesome palace, just as I imagined it would be, with gothic stone spires of gray and black and white reaching up into the heavens, clouded with snow. It cast an enormous stormy shadow on us as we entered.

"So, this is home," I said to Shasta, my voice trembling only a little. Was Kian there, I wondered, and my heart gave a little leap.

Shasta nodded and squeezed Rodney's hand. They had decided that they would do the honorable thing and present themselves to the Queen as lovers, and ask for her mercy and good will. Lying to her, in the end, would only have angered her further; she would have found out in the end, and neither of them wanted to risk the Queen's wrath for any perceived disrespect.

"I'm scared," I admitted.

"Me too," said Shasta.

But we went inside anyway, Shasta commanding the guards to let us pass. "I am not a hostage," she announced. "These are my friends, not my captors. They have escorted me safely, and rescued me from the threat of the dire Pixies. You will treat them as you would treat any high-ranking knight in the Winter Court." The easy imperiousness with which she took on her role as Princess impressed me even as it frightened me; she switched so casually between the giggles and gestures of a teenage girl and the chilling regality of a chrysalis monarch.

"The Queen will see you now," said one guard.

So, this was the Winter Queen – the

woman willing to send her own son to jail if he failed the royal expectations placed upon him. I could not say I was overly eager to come face to face with her.

We were marched into the throne room – it was made of blue ice, and the throne constructed of glassy snowflakes.

The Winter Queen sat before us, pale and upright. She was as beautiful as her children – perhaps even more so – for in her eyes there was the experience and wisdom of all her years on the throne, and her features had took on lines of maturity that even Shasta and Kian could not match in all their youthful beauty, as glorious as they were. She had dark brown hair that framed her porcelain face like so many yards of velvet ribbon; her eyes were blue and pierced straight through me. The Summer Queen had been maternal, if harsh; the Winter Queen seemed implacable in her cool serenity.

She turned first to Shasta. "I am very

disappointed in you, Shasta," said the Winter Queen. "Getting yourself kidnapped. I thought I taught you better than that. A princess should be able to defend herself – not needing to be rescued by knights like these." She waved her hand dismissively towards us. "How are we to be a safe kingdom if our women are not as strong and as able to fight as our men? You getting yourself captured puts a burden on all of us."

Shasta bowed down deeply to the floor. "Your Highness," she began. "I am sorry for what I have done. I was foolish and careless, and this will only motivate me to work harder – to ensure that I stay as strong and as well-equipped to fight as befits any princess of this realm. But I must ask your favor. For this knight, Rodney, has treated me always with the utmost kindness and respect. He has protected me through the many ills I have encountered..."

"A true princess of the realm," said the Queen, "should not need protection."

"If I may," Rodney cut in with as much respect as he could manage in his ardor. "Your Highness, I beg you."

"You may," said the Queen, with a faint twinkle of amusement.

"She protected me just as often, your Highness," said Rodney. "My devotion to her is at once enormous respect for her capacities as a fighter and as a fairy, and yet desire to do what I can – whether it be protection or service – to better her life. I am as grateful for her help in our escape from the Pixie Kingdom as I am for her beauty, or for her intelligence, or for her presence beside me now. And such a creature can only come from the most august of mothers." His speech would have been more convincing had he not tripped on the bow.

"I see you are devoted," said the Queen. "But you are a Summer knight, are you not?"

"I am that," said Rodney, "but my heart is with your daughter – and Summer or Winter aside, I offer her all my devotion as her servant on my fairy honor."

"You speak well, Knight," said the Queen. "If boldly. But my daughter has disappointed me. I will not have her needing to be saved again, although I thank you for your service."

"Please, your Highness," Rodney dropped to his knees again. "May I stay to serve her? I will not ask the honor of protecting her. I ask only to do what she requires of me." He let his forehead touch the floor in a mark of respect.

"You may stay for the time being," said the Queen. "I shall decide later what to do with you." But I could see a hint of smile in her eyes.

"Now you," she turned to me. "Breena, you have fulfilled your part of the deal. It is my turn to do something for you."

She gave the sign, and a troop of guards came out of a door on the right side of the throne room. I caught sight of Kian at their head – looking more beautiful than ever in full military garb – and I nearly gasped; I could feel Logan stiffening behind me. But before I could take in his presence I saw who it was that he was leading.

I had waited for her for so long, missed her for so long, tried to push out the pain from my mind to carry on, but she was there – and with her I was again a child, and she was my mother.

I ran to her and buried my face in her neck, hugging her so tightly that she gasped.

"Mommy!"

She began stroking my hair. "Bree – darling Bree – I'm so sorry..."

There were tears in my eyes. I could see Shasta looking enviously at me out of the corner of her eye, standing straight up with royal poise, and I realized that she must have missed her mother, too, frozen away in the Summer Court, and that she longed to be able to embrace her with as much fervor as I was embracing my mother now. I felt lucky; I felt blessed.

"Are you all right?"

"Yes, my darling, yes." My mother kissed me on both cheeks. "The Winter Queen has been a wise and a generous host."

Perhaps it was better for my mother to be with the Winter Queen than with the Summer Queen, her rival. I remembered how I had feared the Winter Queen in earlier days; I did not fear her now. I respected both of the rulers – both proud, strong women trying to keep their countries together in wartime.

"Very well," said the Winter Queen. "It seems that the exchange has been completed. Our work here is done."

I saw Kian staring at me out of the corner of my eye, his face pale and breathless. I could feel his eyes follow the curves and lines of my body; I turned away and I could still feel him there, and I too could not breathe. I tried to ignore it – I would speak to him. I knew – but for now I did not know what to say. I could not tell him that I was going away forever – with Logan, with my mother, to the Land Beyond the Crystal River where no fairy love could survive.

"I think," said the Queen. "That I would like to attend a ball this evening." She gave us a wry smile. "In celebration of my daughter's safe return, and of a successful liaison between the two fairy courts." She turned to the guards. "You will arrange this, yes?"

They kneeled to the floor, struck the floor with their spears, and headed off in unison. Kian followed them, giving me one last lingering look as he did so. My face was red – I could not hide it – and Logan stiffened beside me. I knew he wanted to be noble to Kian – they respected each other, after all, as soldiers if nothing else – but I could feel his jealousy seeping through his politesse.

"You, my dear guests," said the Queen. "May stay the night – yes, you as well, Rodney.

And you will come to the ball."

Shasta gave me a weak smile.

"I would be honored to follow your requests in all things, your Highness," I said, curtseying deeply. Perhaps I was learning to speak like fairy royalty after all.

Chapter 11

Before the celebration feast was to begin, we were given a few hours to rest, relax, and perhaps most importantly, to bathe. I had not had access to running water since the palace of the Summer Court, and I smelled precisely like I'd been trekking through the wilderness for a week and battling Pixies – I could still smell the moat on me, the dolphins. How had Logan managed to kiss me when I was quite so disgusting, I wondered half-heartedly as I soaked myself in an enormous bathtub, scrubbing every last bit of dirt out of my hair and skin. His devotion touched me, even as it made me wary.

My mother, for her part, seemed entirely at ease in the guest room to which we were assigned – chiding me for leaving my clothes on the floor and for not having folded them. They were so caked and crusted with mud that for my part I would have been happy to never see them again – and paced the room while I bathed – I could see her silhouette going back and forth from behind the changing-screen that divided my bath from the rest of the room.

When at last I had scrubbed every trace of dust and grime from my body, I wrapped myself in a blue silk dressing gown and sat down next to my mother.

I couldn't help it; I started crying.

I had been fighting so long and so hard for so long – I had risked being the bride of a pixie king, risked death and kidnapping and war and creatures in the Summer Queen's dungeons – and seeing her sitting there before me, as kind and beautiful as she had ever been, filled me with tender sadness, and made me realize precisely how tired I had been.

"Mommy," I murmured into her shoulder.

I wondered what the Winter Queen would think of me – acting like a child, an immature child who needed to be saved. Shasta surely was given no such luxury on her return. But it felt good to be sixteen again, to relax for just a while as my mother stroked my hair and wrapped her arms around me.

"I'm so sorry, Bree darling," she said. "I'm sorry I didn't tell you sooner."

I didn't have the strength to be angry at her for that.

"Mommy," I whispered again.

"Listen, Bree," said my mother, taking my hands in hers. "I want to tell you everything – okay? Do you want to listen? Or do you want to sleep?"

"No," I said. "I want to know."

She kissed my forehead. "I came to Feyland because I knew the Winter Queen was looking for you. I knew giving myself up as a hostage would stop the Queen from looking for you. I understand what a mother is going through – I knew I would not be harmed. She may be a fearsome ruler, but she is a wise and kind one – and she does love her daughter very much. When you are older, perhaps, you will understand that; I know she does not make it as clear as I might. But that is the Fairy way." She laughed darkly. "That has always been the Fairy way. But then the Winter Prince came to find you..."

"He was kind!" I said. "You don't have to worry about that."

"I am worried about that," said my mother. "But not because he is the Winter Prince." She smiled. "But rather because he is the first...and the first love is something special."

"Was my father your first love?" I asked her.

She shook her head. "No – not the first. I went to college – studied art – met lots of boys. Even fell in love with some of them. But when I was a senior, I met someone strange – someone different. A student in my arts class. And his paintings were so magical, so beautiful – so different – that I felt that he must be possessed of a special genius, to be able to see a universe so alive with beauty, to imagine it.

"As it turns out, he was painting from memory. So – maybe he wasn't so much of a genius after all. But he was talented." She stroked my hair. "And you, Bree, have inherited that talent."

"What was his name?"

"Well – in the Fairy kingdom he was known as Foxflame. But of course when he snuck into the mortal realm to go flirt with mortal women, he went by another name. He called himself Frank."

"Frank Foxflame," I said.

"Quite a contrast. Now, he'd dated lots of mortal girls – Frank was known as a bit of a womanizer. But then he and I met...and it was different, with us. We fell in love. And after we'd been dating for about six months Frank told me his secret. He was a fairy – and not only a fairy, but in fact the younger son of the Fairy Queen of the Summer Court! And life was carefree and wonderful with us. As a fairy prince, he had few expectations on him – he wasn't the Crown Prince, after all – and after the initial surprise I grew to love Feyland – because I loved him.

"Feyland was different in those days, Bree. It was softer – kinder. And as an artist, I found that my ability to paint and dream and create beautiful things was immeasurably increased by the time I spent there. But then Frank's brother – his older brother, the Crown Prince – was killed by the Pixies, and Frank had to become king.

"This meant marrying his brother's fiancée Redleaf of Autumn – the Autumn Kingdom had recently become a vassal of Summer, and having Redleaf as Summer Queen would help to keep that peace. I encouraged him to do it. It was only an arranged marriage, we thought. He was not required to love her.

"But we were selfish, Bree. We forgot one thing. And that was the chance that she might love him. We never realized it – we thought...we thought it was just politics for her. But she was a young girl in a strange land – far from her home, which had already lost its sovereignty - whose husband was carrying on with a mortal woman...

"And then when you were born, there were more problems still. Redleaf could not bear children – not an uncommon ailment among fairies – but the Autumn Kingdom would not stand for a half-human heir to the throne. And your power was strong – you repelled a kewpie when you were still in the cradle! It was a dangerous power. And then Autumn was perhaps going to revolt...we needed to get out of the way, to let it at least look like Redleaf would represent Autumn interests on the throne...."

Politics! I thought bitterly. Always politics! No matter what, the only thing anyone in fairyland seemed to care about was marriages and treaties, uprisings and revolts and wars.

"So we were banished. It was so hard for your father to do it – I don't blame him. He had been selfish for so long – we both had – choosing our love over the good of an entire nation. And in the end we realized it was best to separate – that if Redleaf could perhaps bear an heir that you would cede your right to the throne, or at least return after years of absence, when the problems with Autumn came down.

And then came the war with Winter..." my mother's voice trailed off. "What a strange life we lead, my child. So strange indeed."

"Did you love my father?" I asked her.

"Yes. Almost too much. More than I loved anything else. A dangerous love. I forgot my principles; I forgot everything. I only felt love –

love strong enough to let me survive the perils of his fairy kiss. But there is someone I love more than your father, Bree."

"Who?" I asked her.

"You. When I became a mother, I realized that for the first time I had to live for you – and not just for me. And I wanted to raise you well, with good values. I wanted to raise you to do what is right, and not what is easy; I wanted to raise you to be brave as well as good. The choices I made were mine. And I had true love – but I also caused a woman – the Summer Queen – great pain. I also nearly risked a war. In the end it was my choice to leave Feyland – and your father. I told him to banish me. Because I didn't want you growing up to learn that your feelings meant more than another's – that your love was so important that nobody else mattered."

"You sound like the Fairies," I said.

"They have a point," my mother said. "But they have magic – and when love and passion are involved, magic is all the more dangerous. Imagine what would happen in our world if everyone in love had magic powers. There would be murders, duels, explosions, love spells – chaos!"

"Chaos," I said.

"So I left your father. I still love him. But in my heart I know I made the right choice," said Raine. "Because I love you more. You are the most important person in my life."

I thought of Logan and Kian. Was I being selfish, leading both of them on?

"But how did you know to do the right thing?" I asked her.

"I knew it in my heart."

I told her about the problems with Logan and Kian; she laughed.

"My little girl is getting so beautiful," she said. "Of course you have men falling over themselves for you. But you're so young! You're only sixteen."

I nodded.

"Here's my advice for you, little girl. *Wait.* Don't feel you need to fall in love all at once. Because when you're sure – you'll be sure. Whether it's Logan, Kian, or someone else – you'll *know*. And don't act on your feelings unless you're sure."

I thought of my feelings for Logan, and of my uncertainty. It seemed so much clearer when my mother said it.

"Why are you always so right," I asked her, unable to repress a grin at the corner of my mouth.

"I'm your mother," she said, smiling. "That's my job. I take care of you." She stroked my cheek. "Whether it's fairies or pixies or boys."

I leaned my head on her shoulder. It was good to be home again.

Chapter 12

It was time for the ball. My mother had helped me dress, cloaking my newly clean body in a gorgeous red velvet dress. I had not worn nice clothing since the dress Delano had given me to wear in the Pixie Castle. This was so much better. The green pixie silk had been uncomfortable – the fabric had tightened around my hips, my waist, my breasts in such a way as I no longer looked like myself; I was no longer in control of the way I looked. This fairy velvet was enchanted, too, but in a different way. The fabric contorted to fit me, but instead of forcing me into the hour-glass figure of the silk pixie gown, this red enhanced my natural look.

"Just like your mother," said my mother, brushing my hair and braiding it. She looked beautiful too, and so much younger than I was used to seeing her. Before this I had always thought of Raine Farrell as my mother, nothing more. But hearing about my father, about her love for him and the difficult choices that she had to make in the end, I began to feel that she was a woman, too – just like me. She knew what I was going through.

"Makeup?" said my mother, as I eyed the pots of paint and ointments that had been left on the vanity. "You – Bree?"

I blushed.

"You're beautiful just the way you are."

"But Shasta will be there..." I couldn't help but turn even redder. "And I don't want to look..." I didn't even know how to find the words. "Plain, I guess."

My mother smiled at me. "No daughter of mine could ever be plain. Besides – it's a masquerade. Nobody will even see your face."

She handed me a mask of red satin, adorned with delicate lace. I put it on, and watched my mother put on hers – colored gold and silver.

"Soon we'll be going home," she said, sighing happily. "And then you'll be free!"

"I don't know how I feel about that," I said. I couldn't lie to my mother, not even about this. "Feyland is...such a place."

"I know what you mean," said my mother. "I miss it sometimes, too. It's like nowhere else on this earth. And when I paint, I always remember what Fairyland looked like, and I try to capture it on canvas. But it's never the same..."

It was now sunset, and time for the ball to begin. The bells – tinkling silver bells – began ringing to alert us to all file down into the grand ante-chamber, from which we would enter the ballroom. My mother squeezed my hand and we walked down together.

The room was splendid. The walls were carved out of glittering ice, reflecting the dancers back in gorgeous shimmers. But magic had been applied to the room – it didn't feel cold at all – but rather as cozy and comfortable as an autumn breeze. Silver candelabras hung from the ceiling, and a gorgeous silvery moon-like orb hung above us, from which all kinds of glittering light were emanating. I gasped in amazement.

"It's splendid," said my mother. "The Winter Court is truly an amazing place."

The dancers were outfitted in a rainbow of colors, gliding in circles and swirls around the shining floor. My feet began tingling; how I wanted to dance! To join in! I knew that going home to Gregory, Oregon, was the right decision, but as I watched the Fairy dancers I knew that Feyland would always be a part of me, that I never wanted to let go of. These were my people; fairy lore and fairy magic was in my blood, more than it ever would be or could have been for my mother. Leaving Feyland would be hard. I swallowed back the tears circling at the corners of my eyes.

"Will you let me have this dance?" said a voice behind me, as a familiar note began to strike up from the orchestra. I turned around. His mask covered his face, but the shining of his eyes gave it all away. I recognized his beautiful, piercing gaze – the eyes that were as blue as the morning after a storm – and I felt his looks bore through me. And then I knew there was nothing for me to do but to say yes to Kian, to give him my hand and let him kiss the tips of my fingers and my knuckles, and then as the Fairy Waltz – that same beloved song we had danced to so often as children – played around us, swelling with emotion and magic, we had to dance with it, echoing the steps that, it had once been foretold, would be playing at our wedding.

I held him tighter; I felt his arms tighten around me. He didn't feel like Logan – strong and rough, warm and all-encompassing. Rather, Kian's touch was softer, gentler. And then I could not remember Logan's touch, or indeed

Logan at all, because as we danced I could feel Kian's lips come closer to mine.

How could I go home to Gregory, I wondered – when my life was here? My love was here? I was trying so hard to make everything go back to normal – to make up for what happened with Logan, to assuage my guilt at nearly getting him killed, to return to the days of Gregory when I was safe and Logan and I would go walking in the woods – that I had ignored my true feelings, my desire to stay in fairyland. I wanted to stay in this world – a place of such beauty, such magic, a place where a fairy prince with eyes like the sea after a storm could take me in his arms for a dance, and I could feel his breath upon my lips as I struggled against myself not to kiss him.

I had thought I would never see him again. Since my time at the Summer Court, I had ignored my feelings, swallowed them back. The Summer Queen had convinced me that Kian and I could never be together – there was too much in the way, too much politics, too much bloodshed, too much hatred between our kingdoms. And yet, with him cradling me in his arms, I felt that our love could outlast and outshine and overcome all of this hatred. I knew then that I loved him, that I could never be happy with anyone else, that I had to stay forever in Feyland, to dance forever with my fairy prince.

I didn't want to wait for him to realize how I felt. I didn't want anyone else taking control – not Delano, not the Winter Queen or the Summer Queen, not Logan – I wanted him to know how much I loved him.

"Come with me," I said, as the dance trickled into silence. "I want to talk to you." I took his hand and led him to a corner of the nearby corridor where we could not be observed.

"Bree..."

I wouldn't let him finish. I took him in my arms and kissed him, fully, on the mouth. Once again I felt the shocks of magic tremble through us – as strong as it had been the first time – maybe stronger, for now I was even surer of my feelings for him.

"Bree," he said again, his voice swelling with joy. He held my hands tighter.

"Listen," I said. "I don't know what's going to happen..."

"I've missed you so much," he said. "My mother knows – she disapproves. She knows you can't stay in Feyland – not with the Summer Queen's banishment still holding...she wants to protect us...with you so far away..." His voice trailed off. His pain was too great for him to bear.

"But it didn't change how I felt. I don't care what the Summer Queen has to say! I want you here, Bree, with me."

"I can't stay in the Winter Kingdom," I said, miserably. As long as I was a royal member of the Summer Court, the political cost would be dire. The people of both courts would never stand for it.

"And I can't stay with the Summer Court, either," I said, my voice filled with darkness. "They won't let me. I tried! But the Summer Queen's anger with my family is still strong. She respects me – maybe – because I respected her – but she won't let me stay. She was willing to let me live just because she knew I'd go off and leave her alone. But if I stayed..."

"Can't you find a way?" cried Kian.

I shook my head. "There's nothing I can do." I wished more than anything that there was another way. "I don't know what to do."

"Go back with your mother, I suppose," said Kian, with some anger in his voice. "To Gregory, Oregon. Along with Logan."

I could hear the jealousy sting in his voice, and it was the most horrible sound in the world.

Chapter 13

Kian and I stood in the corner of the corridor, staring at each other. We did not know what to say to each other. I wanted to comfort him, to tell him that I loved him, that he meant more to me than anyone else, but the words escaped me. How could I betray Logan, who had done so much for me? Who had nearly risked his life for me, again and again? In assuaging Kian's jealousy, I would end up hurting my best friend. I swallowed hard, trying to muster up the courage to speak.

Before I could say anything, Logan walked in. From the moment he saw us I knew that he was angry, that animal jealousy had been sparked within him. He drew in his breath sharply and gave Kian a long, hard stare. I could feel the tension building between them. They had developed a somewhat tenuous partnership

157

in the period following my capture by the Pixie King; they had been forced to work together to save me, and they each bequeathed each other some measure of grudging respect. Even now, although I could see the hatred and anger bubbling in Logan's eyes as he watched the two of us together, he stood up straight, with a noble bearing that befitted his wolf-like nature, looking Kian directly in the eye.

"Your mother is looking for you, Breena," Logan said stiffly. "I hate to drag you away..."

"No, it's fine," I said hurriedly – then caught sight of Kian's face. He looked stricken. "I'll – I'll be right back, Kian," I said, trying to show him my feelings through a weak smile. It was unsuccessful, and a lump rose in my throat.

I went over to my mother, where she was dancing in a corner with one of the Knights of the Winter Kingdom. When she saw me she blushed, then her blush turned into a smile. "Bree, darling," she said. "How are you enjoying the ball."

"It's beautiful," I said. I smiled weakly at her. "But..."

"But what, darling?" My mother curtseyed at her dance partner and took me aside.

"It's going to be hard," I said at last, breathing a sigh of relief as I said it.

"What's going to be hard, darling?"

I took my mother's hand. "Leaving," I said. "Leaving here. Leaving all this. It feels like..."

"Home?" asked my mother.

"Yes!" I leaped up, overjoyed that she understood me. "Just like home! It's like – somehow – I never fit in, you know, in the other place. Gregory. The Land Beyond the Crystal River. Whatever you want to call it. I was always different. I was always strange. And I always felt out of place, like my soul belonged somewhere else and I just couldn't understand why. And then when all this happened...I don't know, Mom – it's like I finally got some answers. It's like I finally understood why I didn't fit in in Gregory. It's like I finally realized that I wasn't a misfit – I was just...not in the right place. And since coming here, despite the danger, despite everything....this is where I belong. It's in my blood. I'm a fairy – as much a fairy as a human. Maybe more so. And I don't want to leave all this behind."

"Oh, darling," she cupped my face with her hand. "I wish I knew what to say to you. I wish I had some way of making this easier for you. But...I don't. I only want to keep you safe and happy, and as long as you're unprotected there is nowhere in the Winter or Summer Court that is safe for you – not to mention the Pixies."

"I know!" I cried. "It's just – it's not fair." I felt so stupid saying it, like a small child, but it was true. It wasn't fair. I knew that my mother had offended Redleaf the Summer Queen, I knew that we would never be welcome in the court, and yet I couldn't deny that I was a fairy – just as much as any of the other fairies – and I belonged here. I didn't deserve to be expelled from my home just because of what my mother had done – as if I had any say in it!

"Life isn't fair," said my mother. "We have to learn to get used to life's disappointments."

But losing Kian was more than just a disappointment. At that moment it felt like Kian was my whole world, and to lose him was to lose a part of myself, to lose my sense of myself.

"I don't think I ever will," I said. "Did you ever get used to losing Fra...my father?" It was still so strange to think of any man as my father. I couldn't even picture what he might have looked like. "Did you get over that?"

My mother's face darkened. "No, I didn't," she said. "And I never will. But I have you, now. And I have a rich, full life – I love my job, my friends – most of all I love my daughter. And these things all make it a little easier. Every day that goes by I remember how much I love you.

And...I might not forget your father, but I can live without him."

I squeezed my mother's hand. It was time to go back to Kian.

But as I approached Kian and Logan, something held me back; I did not want to go further. I saw them standing next to each other, making small talk with obvious effort. But it was clear that the two of them were restrained only by politeness from leaping at each other's throats. I shuffled closer, unnoticed, so I could better hear their conversation.

"You think that she's better off here?" Logan was saying, his voice turning into a wolf-like growl as his emotions got the better of him. "Getting carried off by Pixies or thrown into the dungeons of the Summer Court? How selfish are you? Instead of letting her go away to Gregory, to be happy – to be normal again!"

"To be with you!" Kian spat. "Let's not pretend that your motives are entirely pure either, *sir.*"

"Well, *sir,* at least I'm not risking her life!"

"You are risking her happiness!" Kian grew louder. "And her destiny! She is the intended Queen of the Summer Court – she is its *heir* – and you wish to remove her from that, to torpedo her back into mediocrity just so that you can be by her side…"

"She's better off in Oregon. Who cares about her destiny? I care about her happiness more than you do. And we were happy, you know. Before you came along. Before you came along with your swords and your glamour and screwed everything up for her! If you know what's good for her you'll let her be. If you really love her as much as you say you do."

Was I happy in Gregory? I wasn't sure. I was content, I suppose – my days walking through the woods with Logan, the calm of the afternoon sun – but I wasn't happy. I always felt that there was something missing in my life –

and what was missing was Feyland, in all its beauty.

"Of course I love her!" Kian snapped. "And I'm convinced she feels the same way."

Oh no, I thought. I didn't want to be dragged into this. My mother had told me to wait until I was sure of how I felt – well, I was sure, but that didn't mean I wanted everything to come out into the open. The Winter Queen's favor was tenuous at best, and I was sure that causing a scene was not the best way to get her to like me any better.

"Let her *go*, Prince," said Logan. "You need to let this go, now."

"She is my intended," said Kian. "She was always my intended; she is my intended now. And nothing that you say or do can break that bond between us. Her love is the key to brokering peace between these two Courts."

"But..."

"This is a fairy matter," said Kian stiffly.

164

"This does not concern you, Wolf."

I could see Logan's brow furrowing with rage. He was about to turn into a werewolf; I could feel it. Emotions like these were too strong for even werewolves to control – and I dreaded the idea of a terrifying, gigantic wolf running loose through the party, shattering the gentle calm of the Winter Court Ball.

"Doesn't concern me?" Logan's voice was growing angrier and louder now. "What do you mean it doesn't concern me?"

"You are a Wolf," said Kian coldly. "Your ways are not our ways. Your laws are not our laws. Your feelings have no place here in the Fairy kingdom."

"How dare you!"

I could see the veins throbbing in Logan's neck; the blush of red anger spread like wildfire over his cheeks. I knew he was angry – and I knew he was not going to let Kian get away with insulting him. His whole body – lithe, strong, and muscular – was shaking with rage, as Kian regarded him with a cool and insufferable stare, filled with contempt. Kian was a prince, after all – and like the rest of the Winter Court he knew how to make his enemies feel small and insignificant. I hoped then that Kian would never turn that anger and rage towards me.

"We in the Wolf community," said Logan, shaking even harder now, "do not take kindly to insults, *Prince*."

And I could see his body prickling, bending over, ready to spring into the fearsome guise of a wolf. I could not let that happen at the Winter Queen's Ball – for my safety and my mother's, I did not want to incur her wrath!

"Logan!" I cried out, my voice flying like an arrow through the air. "Please – Logan – don't do this, don't get mad, please!" I rushed to him and put my arms around him, trying to comfort him. "Shh...shh...Logan – control your temper, control it, please calm down." I wanted only to soothe him, to make it easier for him. I wanted him to calm down and return to his human state before the Wolf in him overtook him. I held him tightly and tried to stroke his arms, to slow his heart rate.

To Kian, it looked like something far worse. I could see the pain lick at his eyes as he stared at me, at us, at my arms around Logan.

"Kian..." I tried to explain, my voice trembling with tears. "Wait a second..."

He could not stand the pain any longer, and he turned away from me.

"Bree...." said Logan, squeezing my hand. He wasn't helping.

"Kian!" I said again, but it was too late. Kian had already begun striding off down the corridor. "Wait – please!"

"I see how things are," said Kian, with impossibly coldness. "I understand now, my Princess. You have made your choice."

And he walked away – too quickly and

decisively for me to catch up with him.

"Bree..." said Logan again, cupping my face with his hand.

I couldn't help it; my anger overcame me. "Don't talk to me!" I snapped, and I returned to the party alone.

Chapter 14

The festivities continued on, even as my heart felt as if it were made out of molten lead. I could feel the pain within my chest – as real and palpable as if it had been physical. This was fairy love, I thought, a magic so strong that it could affect the body in this way. I thought of my mother's face when we spoke of Frank Foxflame and I wondered whether she too suffered in the same way, whether maybe these feelings weren't exclusively fairy-born. My eyes were red; I tried to hide my pain beneath my mask but I felt that the shame and agony I felt were too great to be swept away or minimized. My pain was too great for me to bear, and far too great to hide. Everyone at the ball would see my eyes and know how I felt. I felt exposed, naked. I didn't want these inter Knights to know that one of their rival royal leaders was just a sixteen-year-old girl in love. I wanted to go somewhere safe, somewhere where I could be myself.

I went to my mother.

I searched for her among the twirling bolts of fabric – the voluminous skirts – silver, then gold and white like ivory, the most beautiful colors I had ever seen mingling together in fairy dances. I kept my eyes out for my mother's dress, my mother's mask, my mother's face. I couldn't find her anywhere.

"Mom?" I called out softly, but my voice was obscured by the throng of voices chattering gaily as they danced.

I made my way through the ballroom, but there was no sight of her. She was not in the ante-chamber, either. I swallowed and kept looking. "Mom? Mom – are you there?"

She was not by the buffet table – a sumptuous feast of delights that far outstripped anything I'd ever tasted in the mortal realm, even Logan's tasty tortilla cooking – nor was she in the hallway. Finally I caught sight of Shasta and Rodney, who were dancing together at one end of the ballroom, their smiles radiant even behind their masks.

"Shasta!" I said, somewhat uncomfortably. They were cradling each other on the dance floor, lost in their ecstasy and their love, and I really wasn't in the mood to disturb them.

"What is it, Bree?" said Shasta, not altogether welcomingly. I don't think she was in the mood to be disturbed, either.

"Have you seen my mother?"

"I saw her," Rodney broke in. "The Winter Queen took her aside – down into the study."

A lump rose in my throat. The Winter Queen – taking my mother away? Was she going back on her promise to let us go – was she going to renege on her agreement, and hurt my mother? I knew the Summer Queen would have been ready to order my mother's execution on a moment's notice – I didn't trust the Winter

Queen to be much better."

"I've got to go," I said, and dashed off in the direction of the royal study.

"Mom!" I cried out, visions of my mother's torture and execution flashing through my head. "Mom!"

I burst into the study.

"What have you done with my mother?" I cried out, almost breaking the door down in my intensity. "Where is she?"

I heard a gentle chuckling. When I had calmed down, I looked around the room, and realized where that chuckling was coming from. The Winter Queen was sitting peacefully upon a stool, a cup of tea in her lap. And my mother, looking perfectly composed and certainly in no mortal danger, was sitting next to her, laughing gently.

"Darling," she said. "I'm all right. You don't have to worry."

I stood awkwardly in the center of the

room.

"I'm sorry," I stammered. "Your Highness – I'm sorry. When the Knight said you'd taken my mother away, I thought..."

"Really, girl," said the Winter Queen, with a hint of disdain mixed with amusement. "What sort of monster do you take me for?"

"After all that's happened..." I tried to explain. "I know the Summer Queen wanted her dead – and I...I know she was a hostage here..."

"Really," said the Winter Queen. "You didn't need to worry – not one bit. You see, my dear child, your mother and I were just catching up. We are getting too old to dance the night away as we did in our youthful days – I was only one hundred ten when I first learned the Fairy Waltz! So we thought we might retire to a more private, quieter setting, away from all these...sprightly children...and catch up. Like old friends."

"Like old friends," I repeated, my eyes

darting from my mother to the Winter Queen and back again. I realized then how comfortable they looked with each other – as if they knew each other well. As if...*they were friends*.

And then it struck me. The Summer Queen had fooled me, in an effort to convince me to leave the Summer Court. My mother had never been in any real danger – she had gone willingly as a hostage precisely because she knew that the Winter Queen would treat her well. She had understood the Winter Queen's plight – her daughter imprisoned by the Summer Court – and had wanted to help free Shasta from Red leaf's tower.

"Friends?" I said again.

"Yes, darling," said my mother. "You see, I know that the Summer Queen and I have had our differences. But in the days before the war, the Winter Court and Summer were far closer than they are now. And I made great friends with the Winter Queen. Kian was born about the same time you were, and you played together as children, and so she and I became close, too, bonding over our love for the children we had borne. I was lonely, you know – life as a concubine in the Winter Court was difficult for me. I was treated with respect because I was the mother of the heir to the throne, but I was never fully accepted. I was an outsider – and those loyal to the Summer Queen thought me a threat and an insult to have in the house. But...the Winter Queen – Silverbeech – always treated me kindly."

"The Winter Court has always been welcoming to outsiders," said the Queen. "At least we were – before the war. And yet I could not find it in my heart to blame Raine for the War – when she had never been part of Summer Court policy. When my husband was killed in battle, it was Raine who comforted me – despite Redleaf's orders to stay as far away as possible. Your mother is one of the kindest women I know, Breena. As for Frank Foxflame – well," she smiled bitterly. "The real story is that it is the Queens that run Feyland. My husband is dead; the Summer King bends to the will of his wife. That is the way of things."

"I wish we had more of that over in my world," I said, half-joking. I was awestruck by the Winter Queen's power and beauty. She possessed that same regal form, that same icy yet kind poise, that had so attracted me to Kian. I tried to remind myself that she was my enemy, that as a Summer Princess I was bound to see her only with mistrust and hatred, but I could not.

I came over and sat down next to my mother.

"Now, we must be boring you, darling," my mother said. "Go off – enjoy the party! Go dance!"

I wanted to dance – dance with Kian's arms wrapped tightly around me, to close my eyes and lose myself in the gorgeous strains of the Fairy Waltz. I could not concentrate.

"Of course," I said. "If Her Highness gives me leave."

"Dance, child," said the Winter Queen. "Dance the night away – for the night is still young."

I tried my best to dance the night away, but I found such things difficult. As I gave my hand to one and then another of the Winter Knights, hoping to forget Kian's kiss in the arms of the other dancers, I could feel Kian's eyes piercing through me, their flame-tinged ice searing through my soul. Every time I curtseyed or took a fairy's hand – every time I did a twirl on the dance floor or clapped at the end of a song, I could feel Kian's reaction, his anger, his love.

I didn't want to fight with him. And yet I could not promise him what I most wanted to give – my love, the promise that I would stay with him in the Winter Court, that I would throw caution aside and be with him.

Shasta caught up with me after one of the dances.

"You've had an interesting night," she said, coldly.

I shrugged. I didn't want to talk to her right now.

"What do you think you're doing?" she said again, louder. "First you tell me that you're in love with my brother – then I see you kissing Logan all through the woods – now you show up here and think you can waltz back into Kian's life – and then you break his heart again! I won't let you hurt my brother, Bree..."

"It's not what you think," I stammered. But how could I explain?

"Please," said Shasta. "You've been messing with my brother's head – what more do I need to know?"

"I love Kian!" I shouted, covering my hand

with my mouth. I had said it aloud – and when I said it I was more sure than ever of how true it was.

"And what about Logan?" Shasta glared at me. "Do you love him, too?"

I considered. "Yes," I said. "I do."

She scoffed.

"But as a friend," I nodded. "Nothing more than a friend. When I thought he was dead – then alive – I got so confused...I wanted to do the right thing. I felt guilty, because his love for me had almost cost him his life. But ultimately...I don't feel the way about Logan that he feels about me."

"Swear?" said Shasta, her voice taking on a dangerous tone.

"I swear it," I said. "I don't feel about Logan the way I feel about Kian. It's different. It's...special."

"Then why did you break his heart again just now?" Shasta wasn't about to let me off the hook just yet.

"What choice do I have, Shasta?" I sighed. "I can't stay. I don't want to hurt anybody – but *I can't stay...*"

"Well, he can't go to you," said Shasta, her demeanor softening somewhat.

"Believe me, Shasta – I'm hurting just as much as he is," I said. It was true, after all.

"Well, you'd better be," said Shasta. "Because if you hurt him, there is no way I'll let you get away with it. Not in all Feyland. Because I care about my family – and I care about my brother – and there isn't a girl in the world who deserves him. Not even you, Breena."

"Don't you think I know that?" I sighed.

"I'll see you in the morning," she said, accepting the offer of a dance from one of the Fairy Knights. Her strictness was more measured now, but I could tell she wasn't going to receive me back into her friendship until she was sure I wasn't an enemy.

I continued dancing for a while longer, trying to forget my worries and my pain. But I couldn't stop staring at Kian. I would catch his eye and then lose it again – he would catch me staring at him and I would look away, ashamed. But I knew the truth – that I could not live without him, and I could see as we stared into each other's eyes that Kian felt the same way about me.

Soon, rosy-fingered dawn began to spread out over the horizon, and the sky turned a brilliant shade of crimson. I knew what this meant. The party was coming to an end. Dawn had come, and today was the day I would have to leave Feyland – perhaps forever – for there was no knowing when the Summer Queen would step down, or if she ever would. We gathered together, my mother and the Queen and Kian and Rodney and Logan and Shasta and I, and said our goodbyes. I curtseyed deeply for the Queen and kissed Shasta on both cheeks – she was willing to return the gesture of goodwill. Rodney I curtseyed for, too, but I could not bear to look at Kian as we parted. Fear struck me, the fear that I would never see him again, and I could taste only ashes in my mouth as I tried to stammer out the words I knew he least wanted to hear.

"I guess this is goodbye, then," I said.

"Goodbye," he said, gruffly, and I could see the tears stinging at the corner of his eyes.

Chapter 15

We set off a short while after. The Winter Queen had provided me, my mother, and Logan with an armed escort of Winter Knights, who had promised to take us to the Crystal River. From there, we would swim across to our world.

"It's an amazing experience," my mother said. "Even better, perhaps, when you're heading the other way."

It had been six weeks since I had left home, and in that time I felt myself to have been immeasurably changed. What would home be like? After all, I would return to school – to extracurricular activities and bullies in the locker room, to a world without myth, to a world without Kian. I did not know how I would explain my absence, or whether I would ever be able to fit into my new life. Clariss and the other mean girls seemed so far away – the troubles they had given me so insignificant now.

We rode onwards towards the morning.

I was exhausted. I had not slept in days, and while the ball had been lovely, it had also proved tiring. My fight with Kian had taken the smile off my face, and my cheeks were white and hollow. I had promised myself that I wouldn't cry, but as we continued on ahead I found my resolve slipping every now and then, so that I had to forcibly restrain myself from succumbing to the tears rising and dissolving in my throat.

"All set?" asked Logan, putting an arm around me. He had not realized what had happened with Kian, and as I saw the broad, proud smile set across his face, I realized that he didn't know how I was feeling, either. I didn't want to have to explain to him that, even in the mortal realm, I wasn't ready to be involved with him – that I probably would never be ready.

"All set," I said, forcing my face into a brave smile.

"We'll have so much fun back home," said Logan. "I promise you, Bree! We'll make dinner together every night – tacos and tortilla chips, or even your favorite couscous with chickpeas and apricots."

"And almonds," I added mechanically. "Don't forget the almonds."

"I won't," said Logan emphatically. "I promise."

"Will you come back here?" I asked. "As a Wolf?"

Logan shrugged. "It is the way of my people to go back and forth," he said. "But I only need to really come here during the full moon, so that I can be a wolf without frightening the other normal people." He smiled. "They don't know about people like us."

"Do you love Feyland?"

"No," said Logan. "I'm here because I have to be. But my home is in Gregory – with my friends, with you. Feyland is just a place I have to go to avoid terrorizing the neighborhood."

"How can you say that?" I said, with more anger than I realized I wanted to let on. "You got to grow up here, to go back and forth, to be part of both worlds – how can you not appreciate that? You're so lucky – getting to go back whenever you want!"

"I don't know, then!" said Logan roughly. "I guess I don't have someone like *Kian* to keep me coming back."

"That's not fair," I said, but I knew that what I was saying was untrue. Logan's anger was entirely justified.

"Besides, you don't belong here," said Logan. "You're an outcast here – a princess in exile. The Summer Queen will probably live on for hundreds more years – you'll probably never get to go back. You only really belong in Gregory."

"Maybe I don't belong anywhere," I said, grimacing. I didn't want to get into a fight, but in the mood I was in I found it difficult to avoid an argument.

"Maybe," said Logan, shuffling and looking down.

His silence unnerved me. I hadn't meant to hurt him – only to try to force him to realize how I felt, how much I wanted from him.

Before I could apologize, however, we heard the trumpeting of horns from afar

We turned around to see what the commotion was. We caught sight of the familiar scarlet banners and golden shields of the Summer Court. For a second, I froze. Had the Summer Queen reneged on her agreement to let us go safely? Was there to be a skirmish between Summer and Winter factions directly in front of me? I gave a nervous gulp.

But then I caught sight of the white flag buoyant above the fray, held up by a noble-looking man with long golden hair and a powerful, rugged expression. Even in Feyland, I knew, the sign meant peace. These men meant us no harm.

I took another look at the man holding the banner. There was something strange about him, almost familiar – his lustrous locks, the diffident humor in his eyes, a twinkle beaded in the blue of his irises. I knew him, and yet I could not place him. It was only when I saw the look on my mother's face – a look of longing, of bitterness, above all of love – that I realized that looking into his face was like looking into a mirror. I knew this man. He was Frank Foxflame.

He was my father.

I couldn't move. I gripped the reins of my horse so tightly that my hands began to tremble. I had dreamed often of my father – unable to put a face to the idea, or even, for so long, a name. I'd always been told that my father was a one-night stand, a passing in the night, insignificant. My mother was my real parent – my father had only ever been an illusion. But here he was in front of me, half myself and entirely beautiful, his stature the overwhelming confidence that came out of fairy blood, and noble fairy blood at that.

"All hail the Summer King!" cried one of the standard-bearers!

"All hail the Summer King!" came the reply from the other Summer Soldiers.

We stopped short. The Winter Knights made cursory displays of respect, their eyes scanning the Summer Court soldiers for any sign of betrayal or untrustworthiness. My mother dismounted her steed, trembling as she approached.

"Frank..." she whispered, her voice searing with pain.

"Raine..." He stopped himself just in time. "My lady. It is an honor to see you again." He raised her hands to his lips and kissed them.

And then he caught sight of me.

His eyes crinkled in delight – the rough, brash, golden man of a moment ago vanished, and in the place of his former arrogance I saw his overwhelming delight, his joy at seeing his daughter for the first time in almost fourteen years.

"Are you..." he asked me, holding out his arms.

"Your Highness," I said abruptly, dropping to my knees in a curtsey. I didn't know what else to call him.

"My daughter?" He strode towards me and cupped his hand around the contours of my face. "Raine...she looks so much – you look so much like your mother, child."

I could see the tears in my mother's eyes.

"Thank you," I said. My voice was trembling. I wasn't sure how to feel yet. I felt that I was supposed to run into his arms, to hold him tightly and tell him that I was so glad to meet my father at last – but truth be told, I wasn't. It didn't move me. It felt strange, surreal – as if this man were an imposter. My mother had for sixteen years been the only parent who mattered – the one who had taken care of me, had clothed me and fed me and loved me and listened to my stories of Clariss bullying me at school. Who was this man, who had barely even met me, who had barely even spoken to me, who hadn't seen me in fourteen years, to call me his daughter?

And yet I could see how my mother could have fell for him. He was charming, passionate – beautiful, his age only adding to the strength and power of his virile frame. He looked more like a lion than a man, with his tawny golden mane and ruddy complexion, and the pulsing muscles at his forearms.

"Your Highness," I said again.

So this was the man for whom Redleaf's heart had broken, for whose sake I was banished from Feyland.

I couldn't help it. I was angry at him. I didn't even know him and yet already I was angry at him.

"I have come," said Frank, drawing himself up to his full considerable height. "To request, Raine, that the Princess Breena be commended to the Summer Court."

Logan's mouth fell open. "*What?*"

"But the Summer Queen..." I started, before realizing that this might not be the most tactful approach. "We're banished!"

"Need I remind you," said my father, "that *I* have final jurisdiction over all decisions made in my kingdom. For years now I have allowed the banishment, knowing it was the best thing for all involved if...my wife could produce an heir. But she has not. And you are the sole heir to the throne – and you are *my* daughter – and I refuse to let you live in that poor shambles they call the mortal world. She is a princess of the royal blood, Raine!"

I couldn't help but sympathize with Redleaf. She had run her country on her own for years, and yet in the end it was her husband who had the power to overturn all her decisions on a whim.

"But she won't allow it..." I protested.

"Yes, she will." He sighed. "I have returned from my travels. I will be spending far more time around the Court. And Redleaf would not dream of allowing you to come to any harm when it is my express order that you be seated in the place of highest honor in the Summer Court banquets, and that you be treated with as much respect as any true member of the Summer Line is due."

Poor Redleaf had always been of the Autumn Line – a stranger among strange people. What would it be like for her – to be publicly humiliated in this way?

And yet Foxflame's voice softened. "My wife knows a great deal about duty," he said. "She is the most dutiful woman I know. And it is for this reason that I am sure that she will be safe. For she has long since put up with the *arrangement* circumstances have forced upon her. And she knows that you are the only chance the Summer Court has at producing an heir. I will not take another concubine – after your mother – and Redleaf has no desire for me to take another *wife*."

Circumstances didn't force it on her, I thought. *You did*. I couldn't help feeling that I didn't like my father very much. Waves of anger came over me.

So, I thought to myself. This is what adults were really like, after all. As selfish and manipulative and petty as teenagers. I didn't know what to do. I wanted to be loyal to my mother – and yet I couldn't help but respect Redleaf, to pity all that she went through. And here was this man, claiming to be my father, demanding my allegiance and respect by virtue of my fairy blood.

Forever Frost (Bitter Frost Series #2)

I wanted to give it to him. But somehow I knew that my feelings would take time.

Chapter 16

"What do you say, Breena?" my father turned to me, giving a hearty harrumph of pleasure. I knew that he expected me to run into his arms right away, to promise that I would assimilate myself totally into the Fairy Court. And yet I held back. I wanted to say "Yes" - there was nothing in the world that would take me away from Feyland – but I didn't want him to think that I was saying "yes" because of him. I was saying "yes" because of the beauty of the snow-capped mountains near Kian's hunting lodge, because of the splendor of the Summer Queen's palace and the scent of the orange groves in the garden outside, because of Kian's kiss and the music of the Fairy waltz.

I would not stay for him.

I faced my father, trembling, trying to

control my anger. "I want to stay in Feyland," I said, "but I don't think it's right for us to just waltz back into the Summer Court." My voice grew louder as my anger grew more difficult to rein in. "I mean, how's the Summer Queen going to feel – with you just going *right over her head*?"

"Breena..." my mother began in a warning voice. "Please..."

"No, I mean it! I mean, she's the one who's been running the country, right?" I knew from my father's face that my words had stung. I was insulting a royal fairy – the Summer King himself – but I didn't care. The Winter Knights looked on, aghast at my audacity. "She's the one who's been fighting this war while you've been off...doing whatever the hell it is you've been doing? Maybe finding other women – other concubines! Why should she just give up and let you walk all over her when *you haven't even been around*." And then I understood the source of my anger. "Not for her." I swallowed, hard.

"And definitely not for me."

My father's face fell; my mother was biting her lip.

"Breena," he said, slowly. "If we are ever to make peace, we need you in Feyland. We need a figurehead untouched by the conflict of the past – a new leader."

"And how is *your wife* going to feel about that?" I turned away from him.

"I admit," said my father, hanging his head. "I have not always been the best husband. I have certainly not always been the best father. But you must never doubt that I have always loved you – from afar, yes, as the Kingdom demanded."

"You let us go away!"

"I told you," my mother broke in wearily, "I chose to undergo banishment – it was the best thing!"

"But he could have tried to fix things!" I said. "He could have stayed home more." I rounded on my father. "And you could have come to visit, you know! If Delano the Pixie could make it past the Crystal River, or if you could make it in order to go to *art school*, well, why couldn't you come to visit me?"

I drew myself up to my full height. "You know – my mother always told me my father was the other half of a one-night stand. Well, that's what you are! You're nothing! You're not my father. You're no more significant than any stranger she could have met at a bar – as far as I'm concerned."

But I knew as I was speaking from the tears running down my cheeks that this wasn't true. It was my father's face – my face reflected in my father's face – that was bringing up all these emotions in me.

"But Breena," said my father quietly, taking my insults bravely and without anger. "You have fairy blood. And you are a fairy princess, and that makes all the difference in

199

the world."

"And how is Redleaf going to react to my mother hanging around the house!" I turned to my mother. "After all you said about being selfish, and learning to do things for others. Was that just a lie?"

"I won't be there," said my mother, at last. "Our daughter is right, Frank. I cannot stay. I cannot remain in Feyland, an insult to your wife and to all the Fairy people."

I felt a shiver in the pit of my stomach. I didn't want to leave, either. I didn't know what I wanted.

"But she can."

I whipped my head around to look at her.

"Breena – I want you to stay in the Summer Court without me," she said. "As much as I love you, as much as I want you with me – I have deprived you of your fairy destiny for so long. I have deprived you of contact with your father – you mustn't be angry with him, for it was I who agreed that he and you should avoid contact, because I thought it was best for you, to raise you without the problems of the Fairy Courts to deal with."

"But he should have struggled harder..." I said, my voice careening into a whine.

"It is time," she said, "that you come to turns with your fairy heritage. With the other half of the story. If I stay in the Summer Court, you are right. It is an insult to Redleaf, whose kindness has far exceeded what either of us deserve. I will not deny that I still – that I will always love your father. But my place is beyond the Crystal River. But yours, Bree – darling – yours is here."

My face was shining with tears; her face was wet against mine as she embraced me.

"I don't know where my place is."

"What?" Logan's voice broke the silence. "So – you're not coming home, Breena?" I could hear the pain in his voice.

My mother continued. "I want you to know your father." She took my hand and placed it in Frank's. "I want you to love your father. I want you to know that he loves you – that he has always loved you – as much as I loved you."

"You mean that?" I turned to Frank, and in the pain on his face I could see that my outburst had affected him strongly.

"I do," he said. "But – I understand, Breena, if you do not wish to be my daughter right away. It has been a long time, after all." He smiled, weakly. "But will you settle for 'friend' for now?"

I considered, then gave a brief nod.

"I want to stay," I said.

"I understand," said my father. "But please forgive me – although I know in my heart that your mother has made the right, the bravest decision, that she could make – if I do not accept it without bitterness, without pain. I will say this to you, Breena. Your mother is one of the strongest women I know. And she has made the decision that I would have alas have been unable to make."

My mother's lips began to tremble.

"Do you guys...want a second?" I asked, lamely.

My mother shot me a grateful smile.

"Come on, Logan," I said. "Let's take a walk." I turned to the Winter Knights. "Could I ask you all to scout the path ahead."

Looking somewhat grateful to be extricated from the awkwardness of the situation, the Winter Knights gladly left us alone – two couples, saying goodbye.

I took Logan down the path to a nearby clearing.

"I guess this is goodbye for us, too," I said.

Logan shuffled in the dirt. "Bree..."

"I'll always care for you very much, Logan." I began. "And I'll always love you, but..." *Not like that*, I wanted to say.

He cut me off, his mouth spreading into a smile I could not bear to wipe off his face. "You love me?"

"Logan, please..."

"I can visit you all the time, if that's what you want." He gathered me into his arms. "It's easy for Wolves, you know. We go back and forth! I can take messages between you and your mother. You can visit your mother! You can visit me!"

"Logan, please!"

I pushed him away – just hard enough to break his concentration. He sighed and smiled up at me. "You know, Breena," he said. "I've always loved you."

I didn't want to hear this.

"Since you – since *we* – were little – the first time we met. You were in the woods, crying – like a little fairy child, even then. Some girls had been picking on you. Saying you looked funny – because you looked like a fairy. Purple eyes, porcelain skin. An unearthly glow that doesn't look like it belongs on the Clarisses of this world. Yeah, it's true – you were funny-looking. You were different-looking. And you know why, Bree?"

"Why?" My heart began to break for him.

"Because you were prettier than all of them."

"Logan..."

"I'll come back and forth all the time – to visit you. To keep watch on you – and on your mother. And I guess I'll have to fight off Clariss' advances on my own. I'll tell them I've got my eyes on someone else – somewhere far away."

He leaned in to kiss me. I wanted his arms around me – I wanted his friendly embrace. But I knew I didn't want this. I moved my head, just slightly, and his kiss landed on my cheek instead.

"Bree..."

He understood at last.

I took his hand and squeezed it. Like my mother, I thought, I had to make the hard decisions sometimes. And I didn't want to hurt Logan any more than I had to. I wanted him to move on, to find another girl to love in the way I loved Kian. What we had was special – it would always be ours – but it was different. It wasn't romantic. It was deeper than that.

"I will always love you, Logan," I said again. "You will always be my best friend."

"*Friend.*" said Logan.

"Yes."

He withdrew. "I understand," he said.

I reached out, hugging him tightly.

"Goodbye, Logan," I said. "I want us to meet again – and often."

"As *friends*," he said bitterly.

"As *best* friends," I said.

Between the trees in the clearing, I could see my mother and my father sharing one last, final, embrace. I knew what they had would never make them happy – nevertheless, in the strength and power of that one kiss, I knew that I would rather experience decades of that unhappiness than give up on finding the true love I wanted, the love that I saw in Kian's eyes when we danced...

"This isn't just a brush-off, then," said Logan, with self-deprecating laughter.

"Never," I said. "I'll be back all the time – or you will. We can cook together in the Fairy kitchens."

"Promise?"

"Promise."

At last he hugged me back.

"It'll take some time," he said. "Before things stop being awkward."

"I know," I said. "But I'm willing to wait."

We hugged one last time and then joined my mother and father, who were looking at each other with the full measure of years of love.

It was time to set off with my father. It was

time to set off towards a new life. I smiled at my father, giving my mother a hug filled with love and pain. I would miss her, I knew, although I knew I would see her again. I was ready.

Chapter 17

"All set, then?" my father asked me. He put a gruff hand on my shoulder – moving slowly and awkwardly, as if he was not quite sure of himself. I knew now that he was feeling as uncomfortable as I was – he was as confused as I was about how to act, how to behave around me. Somehow the knowledge made me feel a little bit better. I wasn't the only one who wasn't sure just what to feel. We mounted our horses and began to ride off, this time not towards the Crystal River but rather towards the Summer Court and the palace of the Summer Queen.

"I'm all set," I said softly. Even so, I couldn't help but turn my neck around to see what my mother and Logan were doing, to see one last glimpse of them before I traveled with my father into a life as new and as strange as anything I could have imagined. They were standing there, looking at me, waving slowly. I knew that they would keep their eyes upon me until my father and I both disappeared into the horizon. The knowledge made me feel safe, made me feel warm. I was loved, I tried to remind myself.

"Do..." my voice trailed off. "Do you think it will be a long time before I see them again?" I tried not to betray my worry. I wanted my father to think I was brave.

"Maybe," said my father. "And maybe not. But either way – you will know that they love you. And you will know that – if you need them, if you call for them – they will be there. It will be your choice, Breena."

"Is it difficult – going back and forth?"

"Wolves do it easily. For fairies it is more complicated. It requires a form of magic not natural to us. But I don't think that is the real reason."

"What is the real reason?"

Forever Frost (Bitter Frost Series #2)

"Feyland is a strange place. It has a hold on us – on all of us. We fight wars over it. We make it our home. We write poems and songs about it. And leaving – psychologically – it is hard."

"But you left," I said, "when you went to go meet my mother."

"Yes, I did," said my father. "I had a dream, you see. A dream of adventure. I wanted to see what lay beyond the Crystal River."

"And what lay beyond the Crystal River?"

"Your mother," he smiled. "And your mother...she made all the treasures of Feyland look like pebbles and dust in comparison with her. With her beauty – her goodness – her strength. You know – I have been watching over you, Bree. As best as I can. I go in disguise among my own kingdom – but I also went to yours. I didn't want you to see me. I didn't want you to know me. I would glamour as a man in a cafe, as a local police officer, as another child in

211

your school. But I would go to watch you – just to make sure you were all right. To make sure you were happy."

"You did?" I felt my heart beat faster at the news.

"Of course!" cried my father. "You may not have been my legitimate child in the eyes of the gossips at the court – but you were always, *always*, mind you, my daughter."

The horses continued onwards.

"Tell me," I said to my father. "Tell me about the Summer Court. What it was like. What it *is* like."

My father laughed. "The magic of Summer," he said, "is unlike anything else. Imagine life, fertility, laughter, joy, ripening fruits and the smell of fresh bread baking in the morning. That is Summer magic. We are a joyful people, zestful, full of life." His smile faded a bit. "At least, we were. Before the war. Now...now, the situation is more complicated, Breena."

"I see," I looked down.

"Originally, we were known for fertility magic. As you might imagine."

"I suppose."

"But when love and – yes, Breena, sex – became seen as taboo in our kingdom, in the aftermath of many wars and many troubles before the time of my grandfather – then suddenly our magic found itself lacking in the very area that was most associated with our power. Fertility. Women grew barren. Generations died out. We knew, deep down, that much of it had to do with our rejection of love – we heard tell of love-marriages and elopements in the mountains and the provinces, far away from the cities and the court, and of the children born of these unions, but even among the husbands and wives who loved each other in the Fairy cities there were often few children, for their love was controlled – measured – bounded by fear."

"But the alternative..." I remembered what Kian had told me about the dangers of mixing love and magic.

"Yes, the alternative," my father sighed. "Duels in the streets. Young boys in love self-immolating because the fire in their hearts lit fire to their clothes – unintentionally. Married couples having spats that turned deadly. Uncontrolled passion. That was when my grandfather signed the Edict of Tree Hill – Tree Hill is about five miles south of here. Denouncing passion and love as dangerous tools."

"And the Winter Court?"

"The Winter Court has a longer tradition than ours of...coldness. They have been a disciplined society. A far more intellectual society than ours, in many ways. I admit this freely. Their magic is stronger because their scholars are more learned, their libraries are fuller. Their technology is more advanced. They needed no Edict. It was only when we realized that their...dispassion would allow them more political power that we had to sign it ourselves."

"But you weren't at war, then?"

"Not this time," said my father. "But we have always been at war, stopped by the occasional peace treaty or cease-fire. There are alliances. There are even friendships. But they always come to an end eventually."

"But you're all fairies!" I said.

"Look at your world," said my father, gravely. "You're all humans."

That stopped me.

"Our cultures are incompatible. Our ways are not their ways."

"That's stupid!" I said, hotly. "That's why the Pixies are gaining power, isn't it? Because the Fairies divided aren't strong enough to fend them off?"

"I suppose so," said my father.

"You know – I was kidnapped by the Pixies

– twice! They plan to try to marry one of the Fairy princesses – to produce a line of hybrid heirs, to entice one side or the other to side with the Pixies, and in turn give heirs of pixie blood the power over all Feyland!"

My father's face turned dark.

"Your mother told me what you have suffered," he said. "And I am truly sorry that you have suffered it. Feyland is a dangerous place, my darling Breena. That is why, you know. That is why we have worked so hard to protect you from it, your mother and I. That is why I could not reveal myself to you – not really. And that is also why, I must say, that your mother did not tell you about Feyland."

"But...eventually..."

"We realized we could not hide your destiny from you any longer. Your mother told me that you began having the dreams, feeling the inexorable push towards our land. Had you not been brought here by that Prince, you would certainly have been brought here by your own will, your own accord. You would have followed your dreams."

"And now?" I asked him. The sun hung heavily in the sky; the Summer Court palace could be seen in the distance.

"And now, you must follow your destiny. And you will one day rule the Fairy Court."

I shuddered.

Chapter 18

My father and I continued traveling for some while longer. The Knights rode behind us at a respectful distance, allowing us to talk in relative privacy. He told me about the history of the Summer Court, of the great and beautiful things that our ancestors had done for the Fairy realm, about the cloud-capped towers and gorgeous visions of Feyland in its heyday that even the most panoramic vistas of the current incarnation could not match. We began to bond – slowly – in our own way. We spoke a bit of painting, and my father told me of his love of the art, and when he spoke of lovingly applying the paint to the canvas, or tenderly brushing the walls of a cave with his paintbrush, his words resonated within me, and I found myself leaning into him, appreciating his words, understanding him. As much as I hated to admit it, we had a connection. He was my father, after all, and we shared a fairy blood and a fairy nature. He talked to me of magic – something I had never been able to truly share with my mother – and explained to me how it worked. I showed him what I had taught myself to do in the Pixie dungeons when first trying to escape from Delano, transfiguring and reshaping objects, and some of the techniques for gathering energy that Kian had taught me when we trained together at the Winter Lodge.

"Very good!" cried my father. "You are a natural. I can tell you are my daughter by your skill alone."

And I couldn't help blushing.

When we had reached the Cliffs of Gorgon, the last major landmark before reaching the Summer Palace, we heard a loud, shrieking bugle.

For a moment I thought perhaps that it was the Summer Knights, heralding our arrival.

But the sound was eerier than that. It was a high-pitched, frenetic sound that meant only one thing, and one thing only. *Attack.*

Out of nowhere, there appeared a flock of blue and silver, swords and shields – like a flurry of predatory birds seized upon them. I knew the insignia – it was the same wintry crest I had seen only days before in the court of the Winter Queen. But these were not the kindly knights I recognized from the ball. These were seasoned men of war, embittered – scars on their faces and in their hearts. And at the head of the crowd I recognized their leader.

It was Flynn.

I had seen Flynn first when I was a prisoner of Kian. Kian had been kind to me, treating me with the respect and duty due to a diplomatic hostage. But Flynn was filled with a hatred of my kind – the Summer Kingdom – and had longed to bring my corpse on display to the Winter Queen, unaware of the Queen's friendship with my mother.

"The Summer King!" Flynn spat, drawing his sword! "I did not see you at the ball."

Our knights drew their swords, and a flurry of gold and red velvet met the steely cool tones of the Winter weapons.

"I came only for my daughter," said my father. "In peace."

"Foxflame." The word was filled with contempt. "Your life will be the prize I have always sought."

"No!" I cried.

"The Prince may be weak for his little Summer Princess – but I am not weak!"

All around us, we heard the clank and clash of silver – knights battling each other to the death. My heart began beating faster.

"Let us pass!" my father roared. "We come in peace!"

I drew a sword from my belt and held it up before my face, my hands trembling only slightly

221

as I sought to defend myself.

"Peace, Summer? Is that what you call it? Peace?"

Flynn rushed at us, his sword slashing wildly.

"Was it peace when you killed my brothers – one by one – and left me the last of my kin to stand at my mother's side at their funerals?"

My father parried with a single blow.

"Was it peace when you ravaged my village, and burned my childhood home down to the ground?"

Another knight rushed at my father and engaged him in hand-to-hand combat. Flynn was left alone, rounding on me.

"We meet again, Princess."

I blocked his thrust; the sword shook in his hand and Flynn looked up at me in surprise.

"So the bitch can fight!" he said, sneering at me.

I was able to defend myself for a few

moments – enough time to dismount and scramble to my feet, but in truth it was Flynn who was the better fighter. It was clear that he was one of the prizes of the Winter Court, and from his powerful demeanor it was easy enough to see why. He overpowered me easily, knocking the sword from my hand.

I heard it clatter on the ground, and the sound was like a death knell in my heart. Terror squeezed my soul.

"No, Breena!" I heard my father cry, his voice contorting in an anguished howl.

Flynn raised his sword above me, poising, readying, aiming to strike, like a snake before its prey.

"No!" another voice cried out – a voice I recognized, and another sword came down against Flynn.

My heart leaped within my chest. It was Kian!

"You shall not have her!" Kian raged

against Flynn, his proud, lithe body moving with the grace and agility of a snow leopard. "You shall not touch her!"

I saw Rodney fighting, too, felling one Winter Knight after another. I could see the pain in his eyes as he did so – the questioning. I knew what he was wondering. Was *this one* a friend to Shasta? Did *this one* know her – or love her? And yet it was his duty to fight, and so Rodney fought on.

Rodney felled his final knight, and then rounded on Flynn.

"I'll take it from here," he called, and Kian ran over to me, helping me up. In the distance we could hear the terrible flapping and clashing of wings as the Fairies, one by one, revealed their expansive wingspans.

"Are you all right?" Kian hugged me tightly, leading me behind a tree. I could not answer. My eyes were fixed on my father, battling away with the full force of his life.

At last my father felled his man, and I was able to breathe.

"Are these...are these your friends?" I asked.

"Some of them," said Kian. "Others I do not know. But they attacked a peaceful rally. They acted dishonorably."

He pressed my forehead close to his lips. "And," he said. "They threatened you."

"Kian..." I breathed, gasping heavily. "I want to stay. I...I am staying...in Feyland."

All around us, the Winter Knights were being defeated. The few that remained alive scrambled to their feet, retreating in a flurry of wings to the sky. Flynn gave us a menacing scowl, but he too dashed – unable to face certain death at the hands of the Summer Court.

"I know," said Kian softly. "I dreamed of you last night. But it was not a dream – a mere dream. It was a vision. I knew Feyland had claimed you as its own. And I knew...I knew to follow you, to help you." He smiled weakly. "I am your intended, after all. And the magic has laid its claim to us. We are bound by it."

"Oh, Kian..." I could not resist kissing him – his lips, his face, his eyelids and his cheeks. "I want so much..."

We heard a sharp "Ahem!" and turned around. My father stood before us, his chain mail stained with blood, with the proud stance of a paternal lion, and only a hint of a bemused grin on his face.

"The Winter Knights have all been defeated," said my father. "Save one." He put a sword against the tip of Kian's throat. For a moment I felt a flicker of fear, until I realized precisely what it was my father had seen us doing. Even in fairy world, I imagined, fathers protected their daughters much in the same way.

"Who is this Winter Knight who remains?" asked my father in a feigned growl. "Clinging to my daughter as if his life depended on it."

"This is Kian," I said, my voice gaining in strength and confidence. "Prince of the Winter Court. Friend and protector to me. And..." my voice grew even louder. "My intended."

"I see." My father stepped back. "I remember promising to you each other – but you were children then. And in light of the war..."

"He is my intended," I said again.

"It is not your intentions that worry me," said my father. "Now, sir," he turned to Kian. "You have fought bravely and honorably – stopping an illegal raid – but I cannot ask you to the Summer Court. It would be...unthinkable. But I shall allow you to...well...to say goodbye, shall we? We shall set up camp for the night in the glen over there – Bree, join us when you are ready. You must thank your...*protector.*"

With a knowing, if cautious, smile, my father left us alone.

I thrust my arms around Kian's neck the

moment that we were in private.

"I don't want to let you go again," I cried.

He held me closer.

"You won't," he said. "I promise. Not again. Never again."

I closed my eyes.

"It won't be easy," he said, "I cannot visit you at your court. You cannot visit me at mine. But there is always a way. Love will find a way."

He kissed me again.

"Breena," he whispered. "Meet me at the hunting lodge. In three days' time – at sundown. Can you do that?"

"I'll try," I whispered back.

He kissed me once more, the tightest, most powerful, most passionate kiss I had ever known.

"Love will find a way," he said.

He mounted his horse and rode off.

Chapter 19

At last we arrived together back at the Summer Court. The palace stood awe-inspiring before us, the orange light of sunset casting a ripe, rich glow over the shining marble. Was this to be my new home, I wondered? Last time I had been here as a prisoner, but here I was, coming at my father's side, arriving as a princess. The Summer Guards bowed down before us as we passed, offering us gestures of remarkable respect. They touched their swords to their foreheads, their eyes downcast. I was a Princess now, I thought – and I tried to remember how elegantly Shasta had behaved in the royal court of the Winter Kingdom and to emulate it.

I held my head up as straight as I could, walked the way I remembered Shasta walking – as if I were floating mid-air above the throng –

and let my father squeeze my hand to give me confidence. There was nothing to worry about, I told myself. The Summer Queen would acquiesce to my father's wishes. I would be safe here. This was my home now.

But fear rose in my throat as we approached the ante-chamber, where the Queen sat on her throne.

Redleaf, I thought. I hadn't known her name beforehand, nor truly understood her story. Seeing her sit immobile, implacable on her throne, her pain and rage masked by a plastic smile, I could not help but feel sorry for her, to feel sorry for my presence. I gulped and looked down at the floor.

"My darling wife," my father said, lightly. "My Queen." He went to her and kissed her hand; she allowed him to take it, barely even seeming to notice his lips touching her fingers.

"I see you have brought my replacement," said the Queen, staring at me with piercing eyes, full of fiery hatred. "And I thought you were such a good, *obedient* girl, Breena."

"I mean you no disrespect," I stammered. "You are my Queen. I am here to spend time with my father, not to usurp..."

"Your *father*?" she spat, looking up at him. "*Her father*?" She laughed. "You barely even knew the girl! Now, her *mother*, on the other hand..."

I had reminded her of my father's love for my mother – inadvertently – and I could see from her face that this was even worse.

"And now that there is a golden chestnut-haired Summer Princess about, perhaps the people will be reminded that I am but a flame-haired Autumn woman – that I am as foreign as this...this...half-breed. Is that what you want of me, my dear Foxflame?" Her voice was chilling, measured, cold. She did not raise it above the terrifying even tones of polite conversation. "After I have ruled the Kingdom in your absence while you have been off...consorting with your *concubines*!"

"Leave us!" my father barked at the guards.

They marched away immediately; the Summer Queen stood, free now to speak louder, and speak louder she did.

"Leaving me to run a war and a kingdom by myself!"

"I admit," my father said quietly, "that in my youth I have been...indiscreet. I left you to run a kingdom when you and I were both mere children, too young to bear these responsibilities alone. But it has been nearly fourteen years since Raine and Breena left the Summer Kingdom, and in that time I have only rarely consorted with any concubine."

(Only rarely! I thought)

"I have stayed away from the Court for other reasons, which you well know. You have always been the strong one – the powerful one –

and I believed we had an understanding. Your political will – my private will. I would leave you the throne – the throne I never wanted, Redleaf, and you would..." his voice broke, "...be kind regarding my weaknesses."

"Her mother, you mean."

"Yes, her mother."

My sympathy for the Summer Queen began to sour! So, she had manipulated my father's love for my mother in order to gain more power on the throne! This wasn't quite the abandoned woman, scraping together a kingdom, that she had seemed to me earlier.

"I have not been with *concubines* these many years," said my father. "I have been among the people of our Court – watching them, relaying their needs to your advisors, spending time in the real world outside this castle."

"There is nothing outside this castle!" cried the Summer Queen. "The only power that matters is here." She placed her hand on the throne. "And now you want this young strumpet to sit beside me."

"I want *my daughter* to sit beside you," said my father. "And sit beside me. I cannot stay away any longer – neglecting my duties for your sake. I am home now – home to rule."

"And I no longer matter?"

"You are my Queen," he said softly – gently, even. "You will always matter. You will always rule alongside me."

"As your consort," she spat. "Not as your equal."

"That is the way of the land," he said. "I have no control over that!"

"You had control when carousing with your concubine! You had control when coming back here – expecting everything to be the same...it will not be the same!"

"Redleaf, please..."

"I will not allow it!" Tears began streaming down her face, tears of rage as much as of sadness. "I have ruled this kingdom – I have fought wars."

"*Your* war," said my father. "I would have been happy to make peace..."

"My people know the life of Summer. But we know death, too – death and rebirth, renewal and decay – that is my way!"

"Your power is great," he said, trying to be tactful.

"Great, yes," and then she smiled a terrible smile. "Great enough for *this*." In a flash, a sudden, terrifying bolt of lightning ricocheted through the room, shaking the walls.

"Dad!" I cried, my voice escaping my body before I could control it.

When the smoke cleared, I saw my father's body lying prostrate on the marble floor.

"Dad!" I cried again, rushing to him. I looked up at the Summer Queen, shaking. "Is he...?"

"And leave you the throne?" she scoffed.

235

"No, he's alive. For now. He is asleep." Her voice took on an eerie kindness. "He's quite tired, you see, Breena. He's had a long voyage. And he'll be asleep – *for a very long time...*"

"Everything you said, about my father abandoning you, about him being away - it was all a lie..." I tried to process my feelings.

"Not a lie," she said. "Not at first. At first – he did run off to *womanize.* And at first I was forced to run this kingdom on my own. It was only later, you see, that I realized – I began to enjoy it. I could mandate legislation to benefit my Autumn people – now subjugated under the Summer name. I could have my will enacted. I was, in essence, the most powerful woman in Feyland. Why...sacrifice that? Why sacrifice that for a man who never even loved me?"

She rang a bell.

From a passageway I had not seen before emerged a short, toad-like man, with bright, bushy flaming hair.

"Wort," she said. "See to it that the King is placed somewhere...comfortable for his rest. He may be asleep a while."

"Of course, my Queen," he said with a sniveling grin.

"Please..." my voice trailed off. There was nothing I could say to her.

"I think the King's escorts should be sent on another mission, don't you? As quickly as possible! Perhaps up north, to the Pixie strongholds. A heroic mission – don't you think? So brave – so unlikely they'll survive it..."

"Naturally...what a pity..." said Wort.

"I do not tolerate betrayal here," said the Queen. "Not from knights. Not from my husband. And certainly not from you, girl..."

"I didn't..."

"You gave me your word that you would leave here! You lied!"

"I didn't lie – I didn't know..."

"I would have been happy to let you go –

be free – be happy away from me. But you betrayed me. And you will be punished. Just as Rodney will be punished for his betrayal."

She saw my stricken face.

"Yes, my advisors have told me all about that. He will be executed – tomorrow, in fact. Don't worry – child – I won't execute you! You're Foxflame's child – the Kingdom wouldn't have it! But he's "ill" - you see – and I shall rule in his illness. And by the time he wakes up, you *will* be dead. Of old age. For we fairies do not age, after a point. It is only murder that can kill us. How terrible, to outlive one's own child. Unnatural. That is why fairy-human unions are so disgusting, so unnatural."

"Please..." I whispered again.

"And your mother will be dead, too."

"Just let me go – I'll go home across the River – I promise..."

"I don't trust you enough to let you loose. Why should I?" she snapped. "Wort, take this girl to a *guest* room."

Wort seized my arms. "Come on then," he said.

"And yes," said the Queen. "I know about your boy, too. The Winter One. Pity you won't be seeing him again, either. Ever again..."

"No!" I cried out, but it was too late. Wort was dragging me away – down the halls of the Summer Court, away from my father, away from safety...

I was a prisoner once more.

Chapter 20

I did not sleep all that night. I couldn't sleep. My mind was on fire. I couldn't stop thinking about Rodney and his execution – at dawn, the Summer Queen had said. I thought of Shasta – did she know? Could she stop him? I remembered how happy and how close the two had looked, how much they loved each other. And I had inadvertently separated them – forever! My heart writhed with guilt. I paced the spartan floors of my bedchamber and rattled over and over at the locked door, but there was no use. The Summer Court was composed of far better-trained guards than the chaos of the Pixie Court, there was no chance of escape.

The night seemed to go on forever – I was alone with my thoughts, and they terrified me – and yet I never wanted the night to end, for the ending of the night spelled dawn, and with dawn came death. I saw the blood-red fingers of the morning spread out across the sky and then I knew it was too late. There was nothing I could do to save Rodney.

I peered at the gallows being built in the courtyard through the bars of my window.

Please, I closed my eyes and tried to think of Kian. *Please, Kian – wherever you are – help me.* I felt my love for him surge into my heart. I focused all my energy on his face, his voice. We had been able to connect telepathically in the past – I prayed now that we could do so again.

Help me.

Like an electric shock, I felt his voice echoing back to me.

I'm on my way.

Get Shasta.

She's gone...

Gone? Had the Queen's advisors assassinated Shasta, too? I swallowed hard and

241

tried not to think about it.

When the sky had at last been enveloped in a golden, pink glow, I heard a rough, brutal knock at the door.

"*Princess,*" the voice mocked me. "You are summoned to the execution!" The door swung open. It was Wort, the Queen's toady adviser.

"Please," I begged him. "Don't do this! Rodney is a brave, loyal servant of the Crown."

"Just be glad it isn't your *own* execution, Princess. The Summer and Winter Courts cannot intermingle. The people are baying for his blood."

"Because *you* started this war!" I shouted! I had no doubt that Wort and the Summer Queen were at the root of all this chaos in Feyland.

"You will not finish it, Princess," he said, and along with some armed guards escorted me to the courtyard.

As a child I had played here, wandering in

and out of the fragrant orange trees and rose bushes. But now it was a cruel place – a place of sacrifice, of execution. I did not like it here.

The scaffolding had been erected, and a crowd had gathered to watch the execution, crying out horrible slurs - "Winter-lover!" "Ice-heart!" in voices filled with pure hatred. Rodney stood chained on the scaffolding, his gaze proud and resolute.

The Summer Queen sat upon her throne, her eyes terrible and implacable. "Sit by me, Breena, dearest." She smiled her horrible smile at me. "Let's watch the show together." I felt the firm, uncompromising hand of Wort pushing me downwards into my seat. "It will be...entertaining." She looked directly outward. There was no chance of mercy coming from her.

My heart was beating like a hummingbird – hundreds and thousands of short, sharp beats, fear rising in my throat. We had the maximum view of Rodney's stern, kind face, of

243

the executioner's axe, of the shadow of that cruel steel cast over Rodney's face. I didn't want to watch. I couldn't bear to see him die. I thought of Shasta.

Kian...

My love...

Even his voice, echoing through my head, could not calm me. Tears were pouring down my cheeks.

"Not crying for a traitor, are we?" asked the Queen.

"No, your Highness," I said, turning towards her and holding her gaze. "I am not." Rodney was not a traitor.

"We are ready," said the Queen, and the bugle sounded – a harsh, horrible sound.

I scanned the crowd – looking for Kian, for Shasta, for my father, for anybody who could help me, who could stop this terrible thing from happening.

"One," announced the Queen, and the

executioner's hand gripped more tightly on his axe.

My heartbeat grew faster; I could not breathe.

"Two." I clutched my hands so hard that my nails dug into my fingers and made them bleed.

"Three..." I closed my eyes, unable to look, unable to see...

There was a flash and a sound – and suddenly everyone around me was standing – there was shouting and commotion everywhere, voices disassociated from bodies, shouting, crying, screaming...

I turned my face back towards the scaffolding. Rodney was gone.

I saw a flash of black whirling through the crowd – Rodney in tow – and then vanishing, no more substantial than a shadow.

Suddenly another flash, and the figure was right near me, so close I could feel the breathing breeze from its cloak. I heard a horrible slashing sound and then it was gone again – Rodney was gone – and there was blood everywhere and there were shouts and I could not put together what was happening. I was covered in blood – it stuck in my hair and rolled down my cheeks – and then I heard Wort's words, and it all made sense to me.

"The Queen is dead," he said, his voice stone-still.

And then I saw her body, the life flowing out of her and onto me, the dagger lying alongside her body – the familiar seal of the Winter Court etched into the handle.

Kian?

No...

I recognized the blade, then. It was Shasta's knife.

They had gone, now, the two of them, into the dawn, propelled by Shasta's magic...

I saw through Kian's eyes for a moment –

he was here, disguised, obscured in the crowd – he had seen them go, seen them escape to safety...

And the blood was beginning to dry on my face.

"Oh my God!"

"The Winter Court!" cried Wort. "has assassinated the Summer Queen."

The crowd, deprived of its execution, was more bloodthirsty than ever. "Kill them! Kill them all! We want Winter blood"

"Blood! Blood! Give us blood!"

I heard wailing, moaning, terror everywhere around me, closing in around me.

The Queen was dead.

I was the new Queen.

Chapter 21

The knowledge shook me like thunder. I stood motionless as the crowd gathered around the Queen's body, shaking ever so slightly as they came closer and closer.

"Breena!" It was a voice I recognized – one of the servants of the palace. "We have to get you out of here." She grabbed hold of my hand. "Get you cleaned up."

In a flash, she and some of the other servants whisked me away, bringing me into the antechamber and then into my bedroom.

"What's going on?" I stammered, but I knew.

Wort was sitting on the bed, waiting for me – surrounded by the other royal advisers. I knew immediately that I did not trust them. It was because of their influence, I knew, that the

Summer Queen had driven Feyland into war to satisfy her own agenda; I did not doubt that they would jump at the first opportunity to destroy me. Nevertheless, I was Queen now. The whole crowd had seen me alive and well outside the execution, and it would look terribly suspicious if I suddenly turned up dead...

"My Queen," he bowed deeply. "The Summer Queen is dead. Long live the Summer Queen."

"Long live the Summer Queen," came a murmuring grumble from the other advisors.

"Your people want to see you."

"Like this?" There was still blood in my hair and on my clothes.

"No, not like this," he conceded. "Maynad, Thistleflower – have her changed into something more...regal. For the sake of your modesty, my Queen, allow us to wait outside. But we shall see you presently in the antechamber."

I gave him a sharp stare as the maids

249

surrounded me. The door closed behind them, and then as fast as quicksilver they began undressing and bathing me, washing away all the blood, the sweat, the pain, the fear. The soap they used smelled like honeysuckle, and the water was so cool and fresh that for a moment I forgot what was happening and lost myself in the sensation of cleanliness.

"We must find you something suitable to wear," said Thistleflower, and dashed off. She returned moments later with the most stunning dress I had ever seen, made of long, flowing, golden silk. "This was from Her Majesty's wardrobe," she said. "It is yours now."

"Do you grieve for your Queen?" I asked her.

Her blush made it apparent that she did not. "I am a loyal subject of the Fairy Court," she said. "My loyalty is to the Queen regnant."

She helped me put on the dress. It fit me perfectly. I considered myself in the mirror.

Forever Frost (Bitter Frost Series #2)

Although my heart was beating like a hummingbird's and my breath was short within my throat, I managed nevertheless to look the part of a glorious Queen – proud and beautiful. I would be strong, I resolved. I would be Queen.

The Fairy servants led me into the antechamber. There, there awaited not only Wort and his advisers but a whole coterie of fairies dressed in stunning black garb. They were mourning, I knew, but even in their grief they would come to attend to affairs of state – these were the courtiers of the Summer Palace, the most powerful fairies in the land. They all knelt down before me as I passed, gliding over the carpet, my crystal slippers levitating me slightly above the ground.

"My Queen," they murmured, one after another. "My Queen."

At last I reached the throne. Its form fit itself to me; I could feel power radiating from the seat and from the legs.

"We, the people and court of Feyland, crown you the Queen of the Summer Court, Empress of Feyland."

Wort placed a golden crown – studded with rubies – upon my head. From the moment it touched the bristles of my hair I felt its power, the magic of its office filling me with strength so great I felt that I could obliterate the entire palace just by closing my eyes. It was a power of life, of renewal, of fruit growing in the fields and crops warm in the earth, of running streams and germinating seeds. I could feel my soul connect with every seed in every plot in every corner of the realm, and I knew that I was a part of them, now, and that they were parts of me, and that all the Fairies in my kingdom were tied in, inextricably, to my magic and my power.

I heard an applause – studded with weeping and grief – rise up from the crowd.

"I am thirsty," I said, and my voice was not my own. "Bring me something to drink."

An attendant – Maynad – came over with a bowl.

"Ambrosia," she whispered. "The royal drink."

Drinking from the bowl was like drinking from the rivers of Eden themselves – this tasted not like water, but like honey and roses, passion fruit and the freshest grapes, gold and amber all at once. I knew that this ambrosia would make me even stronger. I gulped it down; I needed strength.

I had to face all these people, all these faces. I had to find Kian – to break the spell on my father, to grow the crops, to stop the war, to find my mother...

I was the Queen, and I felt my responsibilities sinking into my shoulders.

It was time to rule.

Epilogue

That night I slept deeply. The proceedings of the day – from Shasta and Rodney's escape to the Queen's death and my coronation – had taken their toll on me, and no sooner had I been able to escape the throng gathering in the throne room than I fell asleep in the new room now assigned to me – the Royal Bedchamber. I dreamed heavily – of Kian, of my mother, of Logan and Shasta – tossing and turning as nightmares overtook me.

But no sooner had my nightmares dissipated into oblivion than I heard a rough knocking on the door of my bedchamber.

"What is it?" I asked, using my magic to light a candle.

"My Queen," I could hear Wort's toad-like croak from behind the door. "It is an emergency of State."

I put on a dressing gown and opened the door.

"We need you downstairs, your Highness. Immediately."

"Of course," I said, glowering at him. I had a feeling there were going to be many midnight "emergencies" in the next couple of weeks.

We met up with the other advisers in the antechamber.

"What is it," I said.

"We have caught the culprit!" announced Wort.

"What culprit?"

"The one who killed the Summer Queen. That foul Winter abomination." He spat.

Shasta! I froze.

"You found the culprit...you have caught the culprit..." I stammered.

"To be handed over for immediate execution. You know how it is, Your Majesty. The people are baying for blood! And now we have caught him."

"Him?"

And then I knew – a sure and terrible knowledge – moments before they opened the door, moments before they dragged Kian – bloodied, bruised, broken – before me. He looked up at me and his eyes were full of pain, full of love.

"A hanging?" Wort continued, oblivious to my hidden pain. "Disemboweling? Beheading? How should we execute this treacherous bastard? The people are waiting, my Queen – they are waiting for blood..."

This was no nightmare.

This was reality.

∗∗∗∗∗∗∗∗∗∗∗∗∗∗∗∗∗∗∗∗∗∗∗∗∗∗∗∗∗∗∗∗∗∗∗∗

Breena, Kian, and Logan's story continues in Book 2 of Bitter Frost

Forever Frost (Bitter Frost Series #2)

Silver Frost
Available Now

Kailin Gow

Excerpt from

PULSE

Book 1

kailin gow

258

prologue

ॐ

She ran like an animal. Her clothes were wet, sopping, clinging to her thighs and to her chest, hollow and transparent around the curve of her shoulders. Her hair shook out droplets of rain; her cheeks were flushed and she was breathless. He could see her heartbeat throbbing at the side of her throat, see it in the rhythmic panting, hear it from across the street, pounding in his ears, intermingled with the thunder bolting from the sky. He could feel it – it felt like an earthquake to him, shaking his ribs, his shoulders, his legs. It had been so long since he had seen a heartbeat like hers – since he had felt a heartbeat at all.

The skies had opened up – as they so often did in North California – without any warning, without any hesitation. It was as if the smooth blue glass ceiling of the world had shattered all at once, letting the primordial oceans pound down upon the pavement. He could see her consternation, her irritation – she wanted nothing but to get out of the rain, to dry herself off, to curl up into something warm and dry.

But Jaegar loved the rain. He loved the energy – the pulse of life beating down upon the earth. He could hear the scattered raindrops in their rhythmic approach to earth and pretend that each fall of rain was a beat of his dead heart. And she was alive with the energy, too – *alive* as he had never seen a woman alive, tossing her hair back, running into shelter, and her lips were pink and her cheeks were red. He remembered that his lips would never again be pink, that his cheeks would never again be red.

She was so young.

Humans so often surprised him in that way. They looked no different from him – he could have been seventeen; he had been seventeen for so long – but their youth never failed to surprise him. The way the world was so new to them – that rain could still take them by surprise, when he had seen so many rainfalls.

He could smell her. The wind carried her scent to him like an animal's scent, and it was all he could do to keep his fangs in check. He leaned heavily upon the branch and parted the leaves to get a better look at her. He could feel the blood – stagnant in his veins – begin something like a torpid, sluggish, shift towards life – the closest thing he would ever get to a heartbeat. She was the sort of girl who made young boys' hearts pound, he thought – and they never knew how lucky they were to experience that sensation.

For it was the physical aspect of it, he thought, that humans understood least of all. They romanticized vampires, of course – how terrible it would be to live at night! To drink blood! To prey upon humans! These were things they could intellectualize, understand. Humans had been forced to commit murder. Humans had been forced to bite back their most natural, primal desires – and so they could almost understand, when they imagined vampires, what it was like to feel that insatiable hunger for a woman's throat, her breast, her wrist. But not a human in the world had ever been alive without *living*, without heartbeat – and so they took it for granted – what it meant, that constant linear throbbing, clock-like, towards inevitable death. For Jaegar was a vampire, and he was not alive, and the dull ache in his chest where a heartbeat should have been was for him one of the most agonizing things in the world.

They don't know, he thought. *They'll never understand.*

He had been told that she was the one. He had waited for her until sunset – the sun agonizing upon him, even with the ring around his finger. Vampires were not meant for light, and even the strongest magic could not take away the pain, searing, burning, aching, in his flesh. He was unnatural in sunlight, and only now that dusk was beginning to settle over him could he find relief. He sat perched in the tree, obscured by the leaves, staring at her as she ran down the street.

He leaned in too closely – the birds noticed at last that something was wrong in their midst and took flight; a flurry of wings beat up around him and the branch snapped from the tree and plummeted to the earth below.

It was enough time to make a distraction.

He concentrated, and in half a second he was behind her, so close he could feel the wind blow her hair

Forever Frost (Bitter Frost Series #2)

upon his lips, and then he opened the umbrella above her.

"Miss," he said.

She startled.

"What the..." She rounded on him.

"You looked wet," he said. She did not seem amused.

"I'm warning you," she said. "I know kung fu."

He had learned kung fu once, many centuries ago. He thought it better not to mention it.

"I'm sorry," he said. "I was just trying to help."

She softened.

"Thanks," she said, lamely. "I'm sorry – I didn't mean to snap at you. But you need to learn not to sneak up on people like that. You scared me."

Her eyes remained fixed upon the tree from which he had come. A suspicious glare clouded her gaze. Had she seen – was she wondering? He knew she knew something was wrong. He tried to maintain whatever pleasant normalcy he could. The sequoias were tall, after all. No human could survive a jump from them – he knew she knew this. He knew she thought he was human.

From Bestselling Author of Frost

Kailin Gow

PULSE

17 year-old Kalina didn't know her boyfriend was a vampire until the night he died of a freak accident. She didn't know he came from a long line of vampires until the night she was visited by his half-brothers Jaegar and Stuart Greystone. There were a lot of secrets her boyfriend didn't tell her. Now she must discover them

Forever Frost (Bitter Frost Series #2)

in order to keep alive. But having two half-brothers
vampires around had just gotten interesting···

About USA Today Bestselling Author Kailin Gow

From visiting Romania, ALA YALSA Award-winning and Million-Selling Author Kailin Gow was asked to write stories about vampires; visiting the Black Forest in Germany and seeing the castles of Europe inspired her to write fantasy; visiting Asia's mystical mountains inspired her to write action adventure and mythological dystopians. From her experience in college as a peer counselor and her volunteer work with women's shelters, she was inspired to write contemporary romance with social issues for women, new adults, young adults, and teens. Having faced adversity, including battling stereotypes and bullying, Kailin Gow has become a well-known speaker and influential figure in media. Her adventurous bold spirit has taken her around the world, where she has ridden on top of elephants through jungles, hand-fed sting rays, studied kung fu from a Shaolin Temple monk, and learned cooking from a celebrity chef. She is a USA Today Bestselling author and has been a #1 Amazon bestselling author over two-hundred times. Her Bitter Frost Series is in development as a TV Series, and her contemporary romance Loving Summer is set to become a feature film. An multi-award-winning filmmaker, director, and actress; Kailin's films have premiered at Cannes, Los Angeles, Rome, England, Paris, Korea, Japan, and even in India's Ministry of Culture.

Compelled to write her first fiction book because of 9/11, Kailin Gow now has over 400 fiction books published under Kailin Gow and various Pen Names in many genres. She is also an award-winning screenwriter, director, and producer whose films have screened and premiered in theaters all over the world including at Cannes. As a speaker and host, she has hosted international shows at the Pasadena Civic Auditorium, been a celebrity judge at beauty pageants, been a judge for writing contests, and hosted television series. She was featured as an Indie Author Success Story on the homepage of Amazon.com for a month and is also included in Amazon's book called Transformations.

Follow Kailin here:

Twitter
@kailingow

Facebook
facebook.com/OfficialKailinGow

Bookbub
https://www.bookbub.com/authors/kailin-gow

Amazon Author Page
https://www.amazon.com/Kailin-Gow/e/B002BMAEH4

Forever Frost (Bitter Frost Series #2)

Twitter
https://twitter.com/kailingow

Instagram
https://www.instagram.com/kailingow

Kailin Gow
Series Reading List

***For Middle Grade (STEM Books in School) ***

Fairy Rose Chronicles - age 13 and up.
Amazon Lee Adventures Series

For 16 and up

The Frost Series
The Wolf Fey Series
The PULSE Series
FADE Series
DESIRE Series
Fire Wars Series
Wordwick Games
Wicked Woods Series
Steampunk Scarlett
The Phantom Diaries
Stoker Sisters
Beyond Crystal River
Red Genesis Series (Science Fiction)
The Summer Pact